Maggie's Image

A Maggie McGill
Mystery

Sharon Burch Toner

Chapter One

The plane's slow descent signaled the end of the long flight. As the ground came closer, Los Angeles spread out below, a giant tapestry, threads of streets and roads interwoven, accented by trees, cloverleaf flowers connected by limbs of freeways, all bathed in bright sunshine from a nearly smogless blue sky.

The Frenchman shook his head and shrugged a most Gallic shrug. Maggie realized that he probably hadn't understood a word of her attempts at casual conversation. His brown eyes held a gravity that caused Maggie to wonder, but they softened when he looked at his bride. She was younger than he and her hazel eyes did not hold the same seriousness. The young woman looked into the man's eyes with a look that was peculiarly French, a combination of inquiry, love, seduction and innocence. Maggie pretended not to see the look, but felt charmed by it all the same.

Maggie had learned only that their names were Andre and Brigitte and that they were on their honeymoon. Maggie thought, not for the first time, that she must find time to learn French.

The plane taxied ever so slowly to the gate. At the first opportunity she stood, smoothed her clothes, and stretched her full five feet to open the overhead bin. From behind her came a friendly, "Here, let me get that for you." A grin brightened the face of the weary looking man as he handed her the tote bag. The fatigue in his face and his rumpled suit spoke of a long journey.

She slung the bag over her shoulder and slipped her hand into the bag's small compartment to be sure her miniature camera was handy. It had been over a year since she'd seen Allie. Since Allie's birth Maggie had been snapping pictures of her at every opportunity and she planned to grab a few shots right away. Her daughter had been the most beautiful baby Maggie ever had seen. Even at ten when Allie had been all knees, elbows, braces and glasses—in Maggie's eyes she never had been anything but beautiful. Through the ups and downs of growing up Allie somehow always rang true.

Up the jet way and there she was! Allie! Medium height and slender, at thirty-one, Allie was something to look at even through non-mother's eyes. Straight, shoulder length blond hair worn brushed to one side, eyes the blue of a tropical ocean under dark straight brows. She was fashionably dressed in trim white jeans, and a blue silk shirt. A pretty young woman, but with a grace and elegance and a special something that went beyond pretty and caused heads, both masculine and feminine, to turn. How Tom and I ever managed to spawn such an exotic creature is a mystery to me, Maggie often thought.

Allie's welcoming smile was wide and she opened her arms for a hug.

"Mom! It's good to see you. I love your hair." The new do was a success! "You look fantastic! I'm so happy to see you," Maggie gave her beloved daughter another tight hug.

Allie hung Maggie's tote bag on her shoulder, "How was the trip? What do you want to do first? Are you hungry? Did you bring many bags?"

"The trip was fine. I slept a lot. Only one bag. I don't care what we. . .. Let's eat soon. I'm famished!"

Allie took Maggie's hand and squeezed it. "I'm so glad you're here." She stepped back and examined her mother. Mom looked great. Five feet even. Moderately round, but not plump, tousled reddish blond hair, eyes still a startling green, a funny soft voice. Maggie's softly draped black slacks and shirt were topped by a bright green jacket that emphasized her rosy complexion. She was a compact bundle of energy who had come through the traumas of a mid-life divorce by returning to graduate school and establishing a counseling practice in the Florida beach community where Allie had grown up.

Across the baggage turntable, Maggie saw a tall, turbaned Arab man she had first noticed in the Miami airport. His well-tailored tropical suit fit his heavily muscled body a shade too snugly and seemed incongruous with the white turban wound round his head. He removed his sunglasses and for a moment Maggie looked into his nearly black eyes, eyes that seemed to look at nothing but to see everything. "Oh." A shiver ran up Maggie's spine.

"Did you say something, Mom?"

"No, nothing." Maggie shifted her gaze around the still empty turntable. She waved to Andre and Brigitte and noticed the tired looking man standing apart and to the back of the crowd, but she couldn't catch his eye.

Pulling Maggie's wheeled bag, Maggie and Allie stepped outside. A long, black limousine waited at the curb. Standing by the driver's door was a swarthy man wearing a turban. Maggie had a faint impression of other figures behind the dark glass.

"Goodness, there are a lot of Middle-Eastern people around here. Makes one wonder! These days, after all that has happened. You know. . .." Maggie commented.

Allie turned, "Oh, well, I guess so. But then, it's a big city. Pretty multi-cultural." She turned back to watching for a break in the traffic. As they stood on the curb, Maggie, struck by how lovely Allie looked at that moment, took out her camera and snapped a quick picture of her daughter.

In her new treasure, a white Miata convertible, Allie pulled a selection of hats from the storage area behind the seats. "Choose one, Mom. You'll want a hat for your hair and the sun." Maggie tried them all, turning to Allie and making a face with each one. Finally she chose a small, floppy white hat with a yellow flower to one side. She pulled it on her head and grinned. Allie put on a wide brimmed blue one with white polka dots. Giggles. Quickly, Maggie pulled out her camera. They put their heads close together and holding the camera at arm's length, snapped a photo.

Top down, the little car zoomed out of the airport garage with a sweet throaty growl. Maggie leaned back into the soft black leather seat, enjoying the combination of warm sunshine on her head and cool breezes ruffling the bits of hair that stuck out around the hat. "I love the car! It is you! Has the new worn off yet?"

Allie shook her head. "Isn't it great? I guess I shouldn't be so excited about a mere material possession, but I just love it. After all, God did tell me to get it!"

Maggie's eyebrows rose, "Really?"

Allie chuckled, "I had this really grandiose dream. God spoke to me. It was a momentous occasion. I thought I'd be told the meaning of life and what I should do. Maybe I'd go to Calcutta to work with the starving or maybe I'd do a photo essay that would end world hunger, or . . .."

"And. . .?"

Allie grinned. "Well, the clouds parted, thunder clapped and a voice boomed, 'Allie McGill! Buy a white Miata and get a Jack Russell Terrier!'" Allie looked at Maggie and they burst into peals of laughter.

Allie turned to Maggie, "There's an old hotel in Hollywood with a terrace where we can eat."

"Sounds good." Maggie gazed at her beautiful daughter. There was an air of fragility about Allie that was deceptive. She had a resiliency that had served her well. While still in college, Allie started her own photography business. After a few lean years, her business began to thrive and now she specialized in photographing children and animals. It was no wonder Allie had taken up photography. Maggie had put a camera in her face from the moment of her birth!

Over a late lunch on a terrace dappled with sun through trellised vines, brick underfoot, a soft breeze, Maggie said, "This is perfection!"

Allie smiled. "I know, Mom, for me too. I've really been looking forward to this visit. Is there anything special you want to do while you're here?"

Maggie said, "I've never been to the Getty, actually never to either one of them."

Allie stretched a little, "No problem. We have two whole weeks. We've been invited to run up to San Francisco, but we don't have to go if you don't want."

Maggie stopped eating, fork in midair. "SAN FRANCISCO! You know I *love* San Francisco. When?"

"Well, there's a study abroad conference up there and we're invited to a party tomorrow night. I don't have to go. But there's a room for us at the Majestic if we want it."

Maggie's voice rose. "The Majestic! Of course, I want to go! What a treat! I've always wanted to stay there." Then more quietly, "But is this business? Would I be in the way?"

Allie shook her head. "Not at all. It's okay, Mom. I'm not really connected with them anymore. They're just being friendly. What do you say?"

Maggie remembered that Foreign Learning Opportunities, known informally as FLO, had hired Allie as a campus recruiter during the uncertain years when her photography business was just getting started. "Well, of course I want to go. Let's do it!"

As they walked from the restaurant, Maggie looked around at the pleasant scene as if to record it in her mind as a souvenir snapshot. Quickly and unobtrusively, she hoped, she pulled her little camera from her purse and snapped a photo. Waiting in the parking lot was a long dark limousine. A turbaned driver sat ramrod straight and motionless in the driver's seat. "Allie, look, " Maggie whispered, "more Arabs!"

She forgot turbans and mysterious men almost immediately because the drive to Allie's house in Malibu took them out Sunset Boulevard which culminated in Pacific Palisades. As they spiraled down the bluff to the Pacific before them, the ocean, sparkling blue, stretched wide to the horizon. Maggie drew in a quick breath, "Oh, how beautiful!"

They turned north along the Pacific Coast Highway, chatting happily, catching up on the details of their lives since their last visit. Their turn off the PCH came up suddenly. The Miata's growl became deeper as they climbed, curving up the narrow streets that created switchbacks on the nearly perpendicular hills. In this neighborhood the houses perched close to the street, close to one another and nearly one on top of the other. Even so, the lush landscaping and strategic situation of each house contributed to its feeling of privacy and seclusion. All had magnificent panoramic views of the ocean. High on the hill, at the very end of one of these streets sat Allie's place.

As they pulled into the carport, Maggie glanced uneasily behind her where the street disappeared off a precipice. At one time the street had continued around the back of the hill to form a loop and wind back down to the PCH. However, during heavy El Nino storms a while back, that portion of the street had washed away taking a few houses with it. Now there was nothing beyond Allie's house but the precipice dropping off into a deep canyon covered with chaparral and scrub vegetation. Each time she thought about it Maggie said a prayer for the stability of the remainder of the street, the hill and her daughter's safety.

Allie's home was a small guest cottage built into the ocean side of the hill, nearly encompassed by huge, old eucalyptus trees. On the carport level was a large bedroom, tiny office and bath. Downstairs was the living room, kitchen and deck. They had their choice of entry. The "front" door was found by going down redwood steps, along a shaded flagstone walk lined with pots of geraniums. They dragged the bags in through the "back" entry from the carport, directly into the office. Maggie walked through Allie's home marveling at the spectacular views. From each room she could see through the trees, over the rooftops to the ocean below.

"Allie, I love what you've done with your place. The pale turquoise and mauve accents are simply perfect against your white furniture and the bleached wood. It's like being in a tree house with ocean, sky and heather colors inside. Great job." Down the narrow stairs into the living room, Maggie exclaimed, "Oh, this is even more beautiful! Those lilies are gorgeous! That vase is perfect for them. But the rug is the best!" She kicked off her shoes and ran bare toes through an extravagantly shaggy white rug in front of the sofa. "I want snapshots of every room."

Allie said, "Thanks, Mom. I like my little house. Someday I'd like to buy a place of my own, but for now, this is perfect. I noticed some new condos farther out in Malibu. Maybe we can check them out while you're here."

Maggie agreed, "I'd love to."

After unpacking and a short settling in, Allie and Maggie walked up the spine of the hilltop from which they had 360-degree views of the canyon behind the neighborhood, of all the rooftops and of the ocean. The air was cool and sweet, smelling of eucalyptus and sage.

That night as she lay in bed, Maggie watched the scimitar shaped moon through the trees and listened to the waves far below on the beach. Lying on this precipice was like being on the edge of the world. She hoped the house would stay put for a long time and thought that life often gives one jumping off places.

Under the marble portico of the Majestic a smiling doorman greeted them. "Hello, Allie. Welcome back." He turned to Maggie, "You must be Allie's mother? Welcome to the Majestic." The welcome was repeated at the front desk. Maggie, impressed by such personalized service, thought it was not at all like a Holiday Inn!

Maggie explored their rooms, a two-room suite. "How elegant! This living room is great. Or should I call it a sitting room? A marble fireplace. Do you think these are real antiques?" Maggie stood in the bay window, "Look, we have a view of the park." In the bedroom she plopped down on an enormous four-poster, but got up immediately to examine the bathroom. "There's a marble tub in here! Too much!"

Allie smiled at her mother's enthusiasm, pleased that she was enjoying the treat.

"Allie, this is too wonderful! Are you sure FLO isn't trying to recruit you to return to them?"

"I don't know, Mom, but it doesn't matter. I love photography and don't intend to change. I've made that clear to them. I think they're just being friendly."

Maggie, in a soft green silk pants suit, and Allie, radiant in deep blue velvet, walked the few blocks to the party in high spirits. It was a beautiful evening. Cool air. Golden sunlight slanting between the tall buildings. As they walked, Allie briefed Maggie on the people she'd be likely to meet at the party including Allie's good friend, Ed Martin, "I think you'll like him, Mom. He's smart and sweet and he's been very nice to me."

"I'm sure I will, Honey. Is he a *friend* or just a friend?"

"Well, we're at that sort of in between stage of relationship where we're good friends. It might intensify or it might not." They walked in silence for a while. "To tell the truth, I really don't know. He's great, but he's geographically undesirable—you know, out of town!"

The two blondes arrived at the party with their faces glowing and a little breathless from their walk. Allie introduced Maggie to Ed Martin, a tall, slender young man with dark hair, mustache and shining brown eyes. Greeting Maggie warmly, he held her hand for an extra moment as he shook it. "Mrs. McGill, I am *so* pleased to meet you. Are you enjoying your visit?"

Maggie smiled back, liking him immediately. He seemed solid and reliable. "Oh, yes, very much. I always love visiting Allie, but coming up here to San Francisco makes my trip even more perfect. Thank you for inviting me." They chatted for a few minutes until Ed excused himself to greet new arrivals.

After being introduced and chatting to several of Allie's friends, Maggie wandered off. Was something inherently amiss with her that she hardly ever enjoyed herself at cocktail parties? It seemed a shame to have so little time for real conversation just when one met a person she might really want to know better. She sipped mineral water and wondered if alcohol would help.

Ed, who was chatting with a tall, portly, dignified looking man with white hair, caught her eye. "Mrs. McGill, I'd like to introduce you to Dr. John Albright. Dr. Albright, meet Maggie McGill. Maggie is Allie McGill's mother. She's visiting from Florida. Maggie, Dr. Albright has been with FLO since its beginning."

Shaking his hand and looking up, Maggie said, "How do you do, Dr. Albright. It's good to meet you."

Dr. Albright's blue eyes looked down into hers and he said, "Mrs. McGill, it's nice to meet you, too. Tell me, what brings you to San Francisco?"

Maggie smiled, "Well, it's a happy coincidence that my visit to Allie coincided with the invitation to come up here. We drove up today."

"I see. And are you enjoying yourself?"

"Very much. It's such a beautiful and exciting city. Have you lived here long, Dr. Albright?"

He cleared his throat, "Er, yes. Yes, I have. Been here for years." Changing the subject, "So, you're from Florida. What do you do there?"

"Oh, I'm a therapist, a counselor."

"That must be interesting work. What caused you to want to enter that field?" He peered closely at her. Why did she feel as if she were in the principal's office?

"I guess I've always been interested in what makes people tick." Maggie gave a little laugh, hoping to lighten the conversation. "Isn't this a lovely party? Have you tried the stuffed mushrooms? They're simply delicious. If you'll excuse me, I think I'll have just one more." Maggie spoke the last rapidly and beat a hasty retreat. My, he was persistent and, well, *nosy*. No, she thought, it was more his attitude than the words. She sighed and headed for the food.

The crowd parted for a moment and across the room she saw Ed greeting new arrivals. Maggie's mouth dropped open! Unless she was mistaken they were the honeymooners from the airplane. What a strange coincidence! For a moment she thought she had caught the Frenchman's eye, but then someone spoke to him and he turned away.

Maggie started across the room to say hello. One of the disadvantages of being very short is that it is quite difficult to make one's way through a crowd. How inconvenient! When she arrived at the other side of the room the French couple was not in sight. Maybe they'd gone to the bar. Again, Maggie launched herself into the sea of the party. Again, traffic was heavy. They were not at the bar either! Maggie gave up and once again looked for Allie.

She found Allie in the ladies room. "Hi Honey. How's the party going? The strangest thing just happened."

Allie turned, "Mom, I'd love to hear about it. Let's bug out and have some dinner in a place quiet enough so that I can hear you. Are you hungry? Shall we go?"

They headed for the door to say good-byes. Ed spent a particularly long time saying good-bye to Allie. This didn't seem to be the right time to ask him about the French couple.

From the party, they walked a few blocks to the Japan Center for dinner. The sun was setting, sending long dusky rays of red-gold light down the now quiet streets. Over sushi and tempura they talked about the party. Allie said, "I think Ed would like to get more serious, but we won't have a chance even to begin if he is in Europe."

Maggie turned a puzzled face to her daughter.

"Oh, Mom. I forgot you don't know. He told me tonight that he's been offered a job in Vienna. It's a great opportunity for him. He's invited me for lunch tomorrow." Changing the subject, Allie asked, "You started to tell me something back there at the party, Mom. What was it?"

Maggie told her about seeing the French couple at the party. "It was such a bizarre thing. I'm sure I saw them. What a strange coincidence! Was it my imagination? I certainly couldn't find them when I looked for them."

Allie became thoughtful, "I'll ask Ed about them tomorrow."

Leaving the restaurant they linked arms and walked through the night back to the hotel laughing, feeling happy to be alive, to be with each other and to be in San Francisco. To

Maggie it felt like being eight again and going on an adventure with her best friend.

After a morning of shopping, Allie dropped Maggie at the hotel and went on to lunch with Ed. Grateful for a chance to put her feet up for a while, Maggie ate her room service sandwich relaxing on the chaise by the window and, with heavy eyes, idly watched the traffic below.

A horn honked outside, Maggie started, blinked and looked across at the park, thinking that she'd like to stroll over and sit in the sun. A young couple sat on a park bench. Two brown heads bent over a book. The couple seemed somehow familiar. "Really!" she said aloud. "This is just too much! Are they following me or am I following them?" Maggie scrambled into her shoes, grabbed the flat plastic room key and ran from the room. No time for the elevator. She hurried down the marble stairs, through the lobby, across the street. Once again, the French couple had disappeared. Just to be sure, she circled the park, looking down each of the streets as she did so. Nothing. "I really didn't expect to find them this time," she mumbled to herself. Drooping, she returned to the hotel just as Allie drove up.

Allie's brow wrinkled with concern, "Mom, you look down. Are you all right?" She asked as they climbed the steps into the lobby.

Maggie mumbled, "Oh. Yes. I'm okay. I just had another visitation or hallucination or something! I thought I saw them again. I know I've been working hard. Could I be imagining these people?"

Allie's level blue eyes gazed into Maggie's, "Mom, you're one of the sanest people I know. If you're seeing them, then they must be there. I can't imagine what's going on. But I trust you. I did remember to ask Ed about them. They are Andre and Brigitte Fouchet. Andre is a professor and is negotiating to join FLO this winter.

They entered their room and plopped down on the sofa. Allie said, "Tell me what you know about the Fouchets."

Maggie said, "Well, they sat beside me on the plane and they were speaking French. You know how it is—five hours knee to knee. I almost felt I knew them by the time we arrived. He was quiet and serious with a thin French face and prominent nose. She seemed much younger than he, not as serious, and she was chattering about 'Ollywood'. They seemed very much in love. Really, they were quite charming."

Allie was serious, "Okay. Let's look at this logically. First, you sat beside them on the plane. That, we assume, was pure chance. Second, they were there last night. That had to be coincidence. Ed said they were whisked into a meeting room as soon as they arrived so that Dr. Sandoval could give them more details about the teaching position. That explains why they disappeared. Today? Maybe just another coincidence. I don't know. But I do know there's nothing wrong with you!" Allie leaned back on the sofa and smiled.

Maggie took a deep breath and let it out slowly, "Thanks, Allie. I do feel better." After a few minutes she straightened and asked, "What next? It's a beautiful day. We're in San Francisco. Let's do some sightseeing."

"How about Golden Gate Park? The Japanese Tea Garden is wonderful."

Maggie gathered up her camera and purse. "Great idea! Let's go."

The Tea Garden was exquisite. Maggie and Allie wandered along shaded paths, over tiny bridges, talking softly, snapping pictures and pausing now and then to sit and contemplate a particularly lovely spot. Each turn of the path, in fact, each turn of the head, brought new and beautiful images into view.

Allie studied a large stone Buddha, taking photos, searching for the best angle. Maggie wandered on, around a turn, along a path at the foot of a miniature mountain of stones and plantings. Sitting on a stone bench beneath the mountain, she gazed back along the path. Just for a moment it seemed as if there were no one in the world except her. The other strollers had disappeared and all sound seemed to have stopped except for the chirping of birds high over her head. She drifted into a reverie, wondering about Allie. Could Ed possibly be the one who would capture Allie's independent and selective heart?

A rustling in the foliage of the mountain behind her caused Maggie to turn quickly and scoot back on the bench. As she moved backwards and to the side there was a whoosh and a crash. She squeezed her eyes tight and when she opened them again there was a large, knobby rock sitting on the ground at her feet. Damn! It must have fallen from that little mountain. It just missed me! With weak knees Maggie rose from the bench and examined the rock. It was larger than a basketball and nearly as round, whitish, granite probably. How fortunate that she had shifted on the bench because it had come down just where she had been sitting. She reached down and touched the white scar left in the stone bench. Maggie's heart beat a strange tattoo in her chest. "Jeez!" Maggie said aloud. "Jeez!"

Chapter Two

Allie ran along the path. "I thought I heard a noise." Then, her voice rising in alarm, "Mother, are you all right? What happened?" She stepped over the stone and took her mother's hands. "Where'd that rock come from?" Allie's face was nearly as pale as Maggie's as she began to realize what had happened. They clung together for a moment, both feeling shaky.

Maggie drew a deep breath and was happy to notice that her voice was quite steady, "Of course I'm all right. I'm fine really. I was just sitting here when I heard a noise. I turned around and there it was! Scary, but it missed me and that's what's important. Do you think we should tell someone? I mean, maybe this rock should be put back in its place or something?"

A uniformed worker hurried down the path toward them. His face was screwed up in a fierce frown. "What happened? Why is that rock there?" He rolled it off to the side of the walk.

Maggie explained, "I was sitting on the bench and it just came down. I don't know how. It missed me by a hair."

The worker became even more agitated, "That couldn't happen. This hill was made to be very safe. The rocks are set in concrete pockets and they have dirt filled in around them. They do not fall!"

Maggie took a breath and drew herself up to her full five feet. "Well, that one did. Fortunately, I wasn't harmed. But you need to look it over. Someone could really get hurt." She took another breath, "Right now I need a cup of tea."

The teahouse was set near the entrance to the garden, a terrace nearly covered with trellised vines, enclosed by low stone walls. Sipping jasmine tea and munching savory crunchy crackers they discussed the incident.

Allie gazed at Maggie with concern, "Mom, let's go back to the hotel. Maybe you need to lie down. That was a scary thing."

"Nonsense! It was an accident and I was frightened, but I certainly wasn't hurt. Let's just forget it. It's no big deal." Changing the subject, "How was your lunch with Ed?"

Allie sighed, "Fine, I guess. Vienna is a chance of a lifetime for him. He couldn't refuse to go." She shrugged her shoulders. "There's no point bemoaning what might have been!"

They finished their tea with the inevitable fortune cookies. Maggie broke her cookie, read the fortune and started a laugh that turned to a croak.

"What does it say?"

She handed it to Allie without speaking. Allie read aloud, "Depart not from the path that fate has you assigned."

Allie grimaced, "Hopefully the path will not have any more falling rocks! One is more than enough!"

Maggie attempted a smile, "Oh, Allie, I'm sure my fated path is going to be just fine—no more scares."

Back in the Miata. Top down. Up and down through the sunny streets. They climbed a particularly steep street. At the top it felt as if there might not be any more street left and then, as they topped the crest, below them spread the city and the bay and the Golden Gate Bridge.

Maggie squealed, "Stop! Stop right here!"

Allie slammed on the brakes and looked at her in alarm. A horn honked furiously behind them. Cars zipped around them.

Maggie smiled, "This is too unbelievably beautiful. I just want to take it in. Can I take a picture?"

Allie pulled to the side. Maggie stood up in the car, pointed her camera and snapped the scene. "Oh, thank you. I hope I didn't frighten you. But it took my breath. It is so spectacular."

Allie agreed, "It's breath-taking. But you did startle me." Allie paused, then said, "I don't understand why people get so upset. Look at that car. He was in such a hurry to pass us and now there he sits. Really!"

Maggie glanced at the small green sedan as they passed. She thought the driver looked familiar, but she'd had enough of people looking familiar. It was becoming a habit.

Maggie was looking forward to a quiet evening with a television movie, when the telephone rang. After a few moments of quiet conversation Allie covered the mouthpiece with her hand and said, "It's Ed. He's inviting us for a stroll on Fisherman's Wharf. Do you want to go? We don't have to if you're not up for it."

"You know, Allie, I'd love to go, but I'm bushed. Why don't you go. I'll probably fall asleep before the movie even gets started."

Allie's face showed concern. "Are you sure? It's really not a big deal. We both could use the rest."

Maggie insisted that her daughter go, saying, "Give Ed my regrets and regards."

After dozing through the movie, Maggie was awake when Allie returned a few hours later. "Hi Honey. Did you have a good time?"

Allie sighed, "Oh, yes, we did. We walked around Fisherman's Wharf and had coffee. It was—I guess it was sort of bittersweet, neither of us wanting to go into the 'might-have-beens'."

Allie's smile was serious, "I learned a little more about the Fouchets from Ed. FLO is courting Andre as professor of Middle East Studies for the spring semester. You met Dr. John Albright at the party. He's taught Middle Eastern studies for several years but he won't be teaching this spring. He's going to work in administration part-time, sort of working toward retirement, I guess. That puts FLO in a bind because they usually have faculty lined up at least a semester in advance."

Maggie looked puzzled, "There's something I don't understand. FLO doesn't have a campus, right?" Allie nodded and Maggie continued, "Then where would a professor teach? How does it work?"

Allie said, "Oh, they're not professors in the traditional sense. They're sort of visiting professors that travel to the various campuses around the world where there are FLO students specializing in their field. They give seminars in those locations. Probably the visiting professors are an extra bonus to the hosting school. But, more importantly, it's a way for FLO to keep up with each student's progress. They hope Andre will accept their offer. He's very respected in his field. Terrorism is his specialty and his latest paper on the subject apparently made pretty big waves among terrorist leaders."

"Oh!" It had the sound of an 'Aha'. Maggie stared at Allie. Allie, her mouth half open, looked back at her. "Do you suppose . . ..? Probably not, but it would explain some of the stuff. Middle East studies. Terrorism. Turbaned men. It does sort of go together."

They discussed possibilities and maybes for hours. Lying in the big four-poster bed, Maggie remembered that tomorrow she and Allie would start back to Los Angeles. Once again the little car would have a chance to stretch its legs and they would leave this mystery behind for a more carefree adventure.

It was a beautiful day with bright sun and cool breezes. Wearing floppy hats Maggie and Allie found the coast and drove steadily south. Maggie sighed with pure pleasure, "Now, this is the life! What a perfect road for your car! I never realized a convertible could be so sensual!"

"Sensual?"

"Well, yes. It's like riding a bicycle or hiking. You become part of the landscape—sounds and scents, even the feel of the air. We have them all. Those are things one misses in a closed car."

After a while, Allie said, "Well, yeah."

Their sporadic chatting was interspersed with long comfortable silences, the kind possible only between people very much in tune with one another. It was as if they could enjoy the sights and the sensations of driving through the afternoon sunshine communally, the conversation between them continuing even in the silence. So that one could pick it up and say it out loud for a while only to permit it then to go underground in silence. There seemed to be perfect communion and perfect understanding.

As much as she had enjoyed San Francisco, Maggie felt relieved to be leaving. She felt safer to be away from the strange coincidences that had plagued her. She wondered if Allie was feeling upset about Ed.

As though her daughter was reading her mind, Allie said, "Ed had tears in his eyes when we said good-bye. We both felt very sad."

Maggie thought about love and friendship, that friendship is not to be undervalued.

Allie continued, "But we'll be friends wherever we are. Having a good friend is the best of all. We'll miss each other, but we won't lose one another." She turned to look at Maggie, squinting in the sunlight. "You know what? I'm feeling happier. I think I'm beginning to feel really good! It feels as if something shifted inside me during the last few hours. I almost feel like celebrating."

They stopped at a tiny roadhouse overlooking the sea and sipped tea and ate enormous slabs of blackberry pie. Back in the car and southward. The sun's rays were lengthening. "Do you want to stop in Monterey or Carmel or what?" Asked Maggie picking up the travel club guidebook.

Allie thought for a moment, "I don't know. How about you? Right now I feel as if I could drive for hours."

"The light is wonderful. I'm not tired yet either. But I don't want to miss any of the scenery. How about driving until dark or until we get tired, whichever comes first?"

"Perfect!"

They hurried past Monterey, purred past Carmel and into Big Sur. The air was like champagne and the whole world seemed enchanted. Maggie loved driving with the top down even if it was beginning to feel cool. They added extra sweaters and pulled their hats tighter around their ears. The surf could be heard from time to time below. A few birds still chirped over their heads and the air was perfumed with eucalyptus, pine and sage. Spectacular cliffs and curves above a dramatically blue Pacific. Each curve brought a vista more beautiful than the last. As the sun dropped lower in the sky the light became more golden, then rosy. Even though the scenery was beyond compare, Maggie was beginning to feel concern because they had come miles without seeing a motel or lodge.

Just before the sun was ready to hit the water, they found a small redwood lodge perched high on a cliff above the surf. They wheeled in, paid the rather stiff rate, deciding that the view was beyond price. The only restaurant for miles around was a tiny drive-in that was just closing. The lodge proprietor arranged for it to stay open until they got there. While the food was being prepared they strolled to the cliff's edge and watched the sun drop into the water and send golden and fuchsia rays arcing across the sky like the fingers of a huge and beneficent hand. The air cooled and quieted, but it still held delicious woodsy scents.

A whistle from the drive-in reminded them their food was ready. As they walked back to the restaurant a small green car rolled in. The proprietor would have to stay open for at least one more customer. Dinner was at the rustic table on their own terrace with the sound of waves below. The last bits of light faded as the last morsels of food disappeared. Allie covered a huge yawn. Maggie echoed it, "It's been a wonderful day and sleep is going to be even more wonderful."

Allie yawned again. "Yes, indeed. Do you want to bathe first or shall I?"

Morning dawned cool and misty. Wanting to be closer to the spectacular scenery, they decided to follow a trail to the bottom of the cliff where the waves were pounding. At the edge of the cliff behind the drive-in there was a small gate in the protective fence with a "Dangerous Trail. Hike at your own risk." sign on it.

Maggie and Allie looked at one another. Being of one mind, without speaking, they opened the gate and started down the trail. They were not going to miss the experience of walking down that trail on this beautiful, dreamy morning.

The steep cliff side was covered with eucalyptus trees, sage, scrub oak and scrub pine. The narrow trail picked its way downward over rocks, at first between trees and, as they dropped lower, among the scrub growth. Allie and Maggie walked steadily down following a series of tight switchbacks. The trail itself was a tiny shelf carved from the sides of the steep cliff. At this early hour they were the only hikers. Far below the waves were crashing on the rocks sending lacy plumes of foam high into the air. Above them were the lodge and the restaurant. But here they were completely alone.

Allie's eyes grew more blue and excited. "Isn't this just great, Mom? I feel suspended between two realities. Kind of eerie, but great!"

"It's magic! I wouldn't have missed this for the world," Maggie answered. They stopped to rest on a big rock beside the trail. "Look at that tree below us. It looks as if it is surrounding the trail." They started down again. As they approached they could see that the tree had grown out and down so that it formed a leafy tunnel over the trail. They snapped pictures of one another in the tunnel.

The trail ended in a tangle of boulders and small scrubby growth. Beyond and a little lower were huge, shiny wet, black boulders and enormous geysers of sea spray. At this level they were unable to talk. Even their shouts were drowned by the noise of the surf pounding on the rocks. They turned and started back up the trail.

Looking up, Maggie shouted, "Look Allie, I think someone's coming down. Look. Near the tunnel?"

They both looked toward the distinctive clump of green that housed the leafy tunnel. But they saw nothing. "Maybe some of the other guests are as ambitious as we are," Allie called back.

The climb up the trail was punctuated with several rest stops. About half way up they exchanged smiles with a young man and woman on their way down. Honeymooners.

When they arrived at the top, they realized they were very hungry. The drive-in was not open, but coffee was being served in the lodge lobby. The proprietor asked, "Did your friend find you? I told him I thought you must have taken the trail."

"What friend?" Allie asked in surprise.

"Who?" Maggie asked simultaneously.

"Are you sure he was looking for us?"

"When?" The questions popped out all at once.

The proprietor, a pleasant middle-aged woman with reddish hair worn drawn back from her face looked confused, "I hope I didn't do anything wrong. It was a man. He said he missed you back in Carmel and that you said you'd meet him here. He seemed nice and he asked for you by name. I thought it was okay."

"We certainly weren't expecting anyone. We didn't even know where we would stop last night until we saw your lodge."

Allie was looking very stern. "Did this man give you his name? Where is he now?"

The woman answered nervously, "Well, no, he didn't give me his name. He was pretty ordinary looking. Sort of medium height, brown hair, kind of quiet, serious. You know, sort of bookish looking. He looked tired like he'd gotten up early to drive down." She was looking worried. "I thought he started down the trail, but his car is gone now so I guess he must have just left."

Maggie forced a little smile. "I'm sure you meant well. Interesting that he knew our names. Maybe he is someone we know. Did you happen to notice what type of car he was driving?"

The woman frowned, "I'm not sure. It was sort of little and green." She seemed relieved to be able to furnish some information that was helpful.

Maggie smiled again, "If he comes back, please tell him you don't know anything. It's upsetting to have someone we can't place ask about us." She was surprised that her voice was steady and that she seemed to be capable of a lucid thought process. With a nod she turned and she and Allie left.

They returned to their room and packed as fast as they could, throwing their things in the bags. They simply wanted to get away as soon as possible. Piling their possessions in the car, they started down the road.

Allie checked the rearview mirror. "Whew! That was *weird!* Who d'you think that guy could be? Do you have any idea? Spooky, too! I keep wanting to look over my shoulder!"

Maggie looked at Allie with more spirit than Allie had seen in the last day or so. "It really is scary. I can't imagine who it was or what's going on. Even so, I feel a little relieved. At least, now I know *something's* going on and I'm not imagining it."

With a glance at Maggie, Allie asked, "You think this incident is connected somehow with that other stuff?"

Maggie nodded, "I certainly do!   I can't tell you how disconcerting it's been to doubt my perceptions and myself.   At least this is something someone else saw."

Allie took her eyes from the road to ask, "Well, what're we going to do now?

"I can't think of anything except to continue as we'd planned and to keep our eyes open.   If, for some reason, we're being watched or followed or whatever, then we need to know who and why.   Right now I can't think of a way to find that out." Maggie made a funny little face.

"I can't either."

They were passing through a particularly beautiful but deserted area.   "Let's enjoy the drive.   The scenery still is wonderful and the air smells good.   I just realized we missed our breakfast back there. Are you hungry?" Maggie asked.

Allie nodded vehemently, "Starving.   I hope we find civilization soon. Check the map. See what's coming up."

"Okay."   Maggie pulled the map from the door pocket, folded it to the right spot and squinted down at it. "San Simeon should be coming up soon. The Hearst Castle is there. D'you think they'll have a restaurant? Is it a town as well?"

"We'll know soon. I just saw a sign. Only three miles."

They rounded a curve and came down a slope.   On their left, far away, high on a hill they saw a stone castle-like building.   On their right was a stone wall with huge eucalyptus trees behind it.

Allie slowed the car and swung it to the right and they were on a shaded narrow road winding between stone walls and huge trees. Ahead on their right were old stucco buildings and beyond them, the ocean. At the corner where the road made a sharp left turn heading back to the highway, was an old stone building with tables outside. "Bingo! I think we've found food!"

They were the only customers on the stone terrace, under ancient trees. As they wolfed down eggs, potatoes and toast, small birds flew down and picked crumbs from the stone terrace. Across the street the brilliant blue of the Pacific blinked between the big trees. Maggie thought it surprising that they could have had such a disquieting morning and still find themselves hungry.

Reading her mind, Allie said, "It was the hike. It's almost eleven. We've been up a long time with nothing to eat."

They sipped their tea and discussed their next move. Should they see the Castle? They were right here.

"You know," Maggie said, "I think I'd rather wait and see it another time when we can really focus on it. I don't know about you, but I'd have a hard time taking it in, considering what I'm having a hard time not thinking about!"

Allie agreed with this oblique statement and they decided to drive on south.

Maggie leaned back in her chair, "This is a charming spot. Very peaceful. The air is perfect. Smell the eucalyptus. Listen to the birds. Look at the ocean. Let's promise ourselves to come back for a couple of days soon." They sat for a while soaking in the peace of the place.

Back on the highway Allie broke the silence, "Isn't it strange? That man came right to the lodge and asked for us and yet, so far, we haven't seen anyone following us. Back in San Simeon we were the only people around. There were no other travelers there. If anyone was following us surely we'd have noticed them."

Maggie agreed, "It has a hit-and-run feeling. In a way, that makes it even scarier because there is nothing we can grab hold of. There is no way we can defend ourselves. We really don't even know if we should be afraid."

At Morro Bay with its picturesque rock sitting like a huge thumb in the middle of the bay they left the coast and turned toward San Luis Obispo. They found themselves looking for small green cars and staring at each one that passed.

"Oh, my gosh!" Maggie gasped, "Do you remember that green car in San Francisco? You know, when I wanted the photo on top of that hill. You stopped the car suddenly and a green car tooted and passed us. Remember? That guy went ahead and then *he* stopped at the side of the street. I thought he looked sort of familiar. I've just remembered. I think he may have been the man who sat behind me on the plane. He looked tired. On the plane, I mean."

Allie's head jerked around, "Mom, are you sure? If that's so then this whole thing is becoming even more mysterious." Allie paused, "If it's possible."

"I think so." Maggie frowned, thinking about the man on the plane. "Yes, I'm pretty sure it was him."

Allie wrinkled her brow. "I keep trying to think of some logical explanation for all of this. D'you have any ideas?"

"Let's see. Maybe there's a big oil deal pending. Maybe they think we know someone who could help them put it through."

"Them who?'

"I don't know. Them."

"How about, the Foucets want you to be the Godmother for their first child?"

"Maybe they're making a movie of Scherezade and they've spotted you for the title role."

"Wrong color hair!"

"Great music!"

"Maybe I'm an Arabian princess, long lost, of course! An heiress! And. . .."

They spent the next hour letting their imaginations run and postulating possible scenarios. At the end their stories became so wild and silly that they burst out laughing. "Well, whatever's going on I hope we find out soon. The suspense is too much."

"I don't think that guy meant to hurt us," Allie sounded serious. "He had a chance when we were alone on the trail." She frowned. "Do you think he's the man we saw by the tunnel?"

Maggie nodded. "I hadn't thought of it, but it's possible."

As they merged into the heavy traffic of Route 101, they realized their quiet drive was over. There were many cars to examine now, even many green cars. A heavy black sedan pulled up close behind them. So close that Allie thought it intended to pass, but then it fell back a few car lengths and remained there matching the speed of the white convertible.

Maggie noticed the big car also. Neither of them mentioned it. It remained there, somehow ominous and yet doing nothing out of the ordinary. Both breathed a sigh of relief when they took an off ramp in Santa Barbara and the big black car sailed right on by. "Whew," came simultaneously from both of them. They looked at one another and laughed.

The Miata wound around the curves of the PCH nearing home. The floppy hats came off as they approached Malibu. The sun was much too low to warrant them. Long fingers of light slanted across the highway and into the car giving a warm glow to everything it touched.

The turn-off and then up the narrow streets, along the switchbacks and home. Home, just in time to see the sun drop into the ocean and the light change from gold to a brilliant rose. Stiffly they unloaded the car and dumped their things in Allie's bedroom.

Maggie stretched her arms above her head, "How about a walk? Just a little one. I feel stiff after our ride and a little exercise helps clear the mind."

"Sounds good to me. We've had quite a day. It seems like three weeks since we hiked this morning." Allie picked up sweaters and off they went.

The hills were alive with the sunset's red light. From the trail above the house they looked down across the rooftops of the neighborhood to the coast highway and the Pacific. Here and there they could catch glimpses of the neighborhood streets winding up the hillside through the area. Silently they watched the top of a small green automobile as it climbed steadily upward.

Without a word they scrambled down to a street and started through the twilight toward their house. The evening was quiet and they could hear the sounds of the Pacific far below. As usual the streets were lined with parked cars, but oddly enough there was no green car anywhere. As they turned the last corner heading for home they passed a florist's van parked at the curb. "Think we're getting flowers?" Allie asked.

Querulously Maggie asked, "That car was green, wasn't it?"

Allie said grimly, "Oh yes, it was green. I don't know how it disappeared. It must have been one of the neighbors who put it in their garage. There are a lot of cars in this neighborhood. I don't pay that much attention to them. I don't recall a green one up here, but certainly there could be one that belongs here that I just don't remember."

Sitting on the deck, sipping herb tea and watching the last traces of red fade from the western sky they discussed the adventures of the day. Allie leaned back, "You know, I certainly am puzzled by what's happened today, but I can't feel very frightened about it. We've not been threatened in any way. Aside from that man's looking for us this morning, nothing unusual has happened. That green car. How many cars do you suppose there are in Los Angeles? How many green ones? If we get upset every time we see a green car, we could be shrink customers in no time." A pause, then, "No offense, Mom!"

Maggie nodded. "You have a point. I think something out of the ordinary is happening. But as you say, we've not been threatened in the least. Maybe we're on the edge of some occurrence that seems strange because we don't know the whole story. It may be a tempest in a teapot. At any rate, I don't intend to let it spoil my visit with you. I came to be with you and to have fun and as far as I'm concerned that's the next order of business!"

A breeze came up and as they watched, clouds drifted across the moon. Allie shivered and pulled her sweater tighter. "Sounds good to me. It looks like it could rain. Unusual for this time of year. Hope we don't lose our good weather."

"Me too. Let's call it a day."

As she lay in bed, Maggie listened to the first light raindrops falling outside, sniffed the clean smell of the new rain drifting in the open window. The gentle rain brought intensified scents of trees and blossoms. Like living in an herb garden Maggie thought. The events of the day floated through her awareness softly, a kaleidoscope of the places and people, sounds and scents. She remembered stepping off the precipice to begin their hike to the rocks below, breakfast under the trees at San Simeon. What would tomorrow bring?

Chapter Three

Maggie woke from a dream of dark turbaned men riding on giant green frogs that leaped over a scimitar shaped moon. She sat up suddenly and said, "What happened to the Arabs?"

From upstairs came Allie's sleepy voice, "Did you say something? Are you awake? I'm not."

"No, no. Stay asleep. I was just dreaming." However, she found she could not go back to sleep. The light was dim, but when she looked at her watch, Maggie discovered it was nearly eight o'clock.

Outside a heavy fog encased everything. Maggie rose and folded up the sofa bed. Tiptoeing, she found a heavy robe on the bathroom door, put it on, and made tea. She sat on the sofa sipping Earl Gray and thinking about the events since she left Florida. What had happened to the dark turbaned men and their limos?

The phone broke her musings. She put down the cold tea and answered.

"Allie? Oh, is that you, Mrs. McGill. This is Ed Martin. I have the most distressing news. Is Allie there?" Ed was speaking rapidly and loudly.

"Hello, Ed. Yes, she's here. Just a moment." Calling upstairs, "Allie, it's Ed.

Allie picked up her bedside phone, "Hello, Ed. What's up?" Sleep still in her voice.

"I think it's best if I speak to both of you. Stay on the line, Mrs. McGill. I have some distressing news. Brigitte Fouchet is missing."

"Missing?"

"How? What? When?" Allie sounded more awake now.

Ed's concern could be heard in his voice. "I don't have all the details, but apparently Brigitte left their hotel in San Francisco to do some shopping. That was yesterday and she still hasn't returned. They haven't any idea what's happened to her or where she may be. Andre is beside himself. They're very much in love. This was their honeymoon, after all. She went out for a short shopping trip and that was the last time she was seen. No one knows more."

"Oh, how dreadful! Poor Andre!" Maggie was remembering the honeymoon couple on the plane, remembering how happy they seemed, how much in love.

"Have the police been contacted? What do they say? Do they have a plan?" Allie asked.

Ed answered, "Yes, they called the police when she hadn't returned for dinner. But the police weren't particularly helpful. I guess she hadn't been gone long enough for them to intervene; however, I believe now they're doing the standard missing person stuff. Not much comfort for Andre. He's gone all silent and morose. Besides being tragically sad, this is embarrassing. As if it weren't enough, the Fouchets' room was broken into

Saturday night while they were at the conference. Nothing was taken, but the room was pretty messed up."

Allie came downstairs, wrapped in a blanket, the cordless phone pressed against her ear. She looked at Maggie and raised her eyebrows. Maggie shrugged and nodded her consent.

"Ed, something sort of weird happened to us yesterday. I don't know how there could be a connection with your news, but here it is." Allie gave Ed a bare bones account of yesterday's adventure. "We're seeing green cars every time we turn around. Strange, huh? We can't decide whether we need to be concerned or not."

Briefly Maggie told Ed about what she was beginning to think of as her turban experiences. "As I was waking up this morning I was wondering what had happened to the Arabs. We haven't seen a turban for a couple of days. I'm not complaining, but I was wondering about it this morning. And now that Brigitte is missing, well, I just sort of wonder . . ." Maggie stopped, not sure what to say next. "Do you think there possibly could be any connection?"

"We don't have a clear picture yet, do we? But, it sort of fits together." Ed said.

"Ed, is there anything we can do for Andre? I feel so badly for him. What a dreadful thing to have happened! I understand what you're saying. I feel embarrassed, too."

Ed's deep voice said, "We're doing what little can be done. Of course, Andre insists on staying in his hotel room, hoping she will call. Hopefully, the police will turn up something soon. In the meantime, you two should keep your eyes open and take care of yourselves."

Andre Fouchet sat on the edge of the hotel bed, his head in his hands. He could not recall ever before feeling so frightened and angry and impotent. Brigitte. He would never forgive himself if Brigitte were . . .. He could not bear even to think of her being frightened or hurt. The telephone interrupted his thoughts. He grabbed it, a drowning man going down, "Yes?"

The voice, speaking English, was cold, no emotion, little inflection and just a trace of an accent, "Doctor Fouchet, listen very carefully. Listen. Do not speak. You are meddling in things that do not concern you. We want you to return to France. You can resume teaching there. Forget the job here. We will help you return. We have something you want. Your wife. If you want to see her again, do exactly as I say. Ask no questions and do not deviate from my instructions. Tell no one about this call. This afternoon at 3:30 exactly, leave your hotel and go to the St. Joseph Hotel. Just beyond the lobby you will see a bank of telephone booths. At exactly 4:15 go to the fourth from the last and wait. You will receive further instructions. Remember. Tell no one."

"Wait. What about Brigitte? Is she all right? Where is she? How do I know she is okay?"

A frightened small voice in French, "Andre, oh Andre. I am so frightened. Andre, I . . .." Brigitte broke off with a gasp!

Cold, impersonal and infinitely frightening, the voice said, "Remember, if you want to see her again. Do as I say. And tell no one!"

"If anything happens to her I'll . . .." Andre shouted as the connection was broken. He dropped the telephone and began to pace rapidly up and down and in circles around the room pounding his fist against the palm of the other hand. *Merde!* What am I to do? Brigitte, Brigitte. . .." Then, gradually his pace slowed and he began to think as he walked slowly around the room, not seeing, not hearing, but focused interiorly, beginning to plan and to hope again.

Andre did not hear the first few knocks, but finally he was pulled from deep thought by insistent knocking at the door. He stopped pacing, straightened, ran his fingers through his hair and straightened his clothes. He walked over and opened the door.

"Dr. Fouchet?" A tall, slender man in a rumpled gray suit asked. "My name is John Landis. I'd like to talk to you about an important matter. May I come in?" The man seemed courteous, almost reticent; however, there was a quality about him that made it difficult for Andre to refuse. Andre ushered him into the room, and motioned for him to sit in one of the two easy chairs. Andre took the other chair and waited.

"Dr. Fouchet, could you tell me where your wife is?"

"She went out shopping. Why do you want to know?"

"Now, Dr. Fouchet, we know from the missing persons report you filed that she left the hotel almost 48 hours ago and that you haven't heard from her since. I'd like you to know that I, uh, we, deeply regret what's happened. I know you must be very concerned." John Landis' gray eyes were sad and apologetic. "Do you have any idea where she may have gone?"

"Who are you? How do you know this information? Why do you want to know?" Andre's accent became more pronounced.

Landis shifted in the chair and pulled a small leather case from his inside pocket. He handed it to Andre, "I'm with the CIA and we would like to help you find your wife."

"Why? Why has the CIA concerned itself with two ordinary French citizens on vacation?" Andre asked cautiously. "What can you do anyway?"

John Landis smiled apologetically and said, "You see, it's like this . . .."

By noon the fog had lifted and the sun shone brightly. Allie was in her office, catching up on photography business and Maggie lounged lazily on the deck. Blissfully, she watched the breeze ruffle the leaves high overhead in the giant eucalyptus tree that sheltered Allie's home. Beyond the leaves the sky was intensely blue. A bird was chattering high above her but she couldn't locate it. Allie stepped out. Maggie murmured, "There must be some way to do this for a living and work every now and then just for fun!"

Allie laughed. "If you figure it out, let me know. I'll sign up! Speaking of work, I have to run in to Westwood to the lab. They've messed up some of the proofs and I need to get it straightened out. Those proofs should go out today. Want to go along?"

"Sure," Maggie stretched and got up.

While Allie straightened out the problem at the lab, Maggie strolled around Westwood, peering into shops. She wandered into a large and cavernous art gallery. After the bright sunlight it took her eyes a moment to adjust to the dimmer interior. The young woman clerk smiled and greeted Maggie. The front part of the gallery was hung with original paintings. Rather too loud and abstract for Maggie's taste.

The rear of the gallery had racks of prints. Flipping through them, Maggie lost awareness of where she was, even of time passing. She was startled when she became aware of the large man standing beside and just a little behind her. She could smell the heavy scent of his cologne. Really, why was he standing so close! Not at all polite! As she turned to speak to him, she saw black eyes staring coldly at her out of a bearded swarthy face. In accented English he said, "Mrs. McGill, you must stay out of things that do not concern you. Give us the picture. Forget the French couple. Go home. You have been warned." He turned and walked rapidly to the rear of the gallery and was gone.

"What? Who are you?" Maggie demanded. "What do you mean? Come back here *at once!"* But he was gone. She looked for a clerk, but saw no one. Maggie hurried through the gallery and out onto the street.

She ran up to the clerk who was chatting with a young man and asked, "Who was that man who was in the gallery?"

The clerk looked confused and shook her head, "What man? What do you mean? Is something wrong?"

"There was a man in the gallery and then he left through the back!"

"No. We don't permit people to come and go through the back. You must be mistaken." The young woman shook her head again.

Maggie's voice quivered as she tried to explain the situation to the clerk, "Well, there certainly was someone, a bearded dark man, and he left through the back. I don't know how he got there. I just looked up and there he was!"

The clerk looked doubtfully at Maggie, "I don't know how he could have got in. I've been here. No one went in except you. It's been a quiet afternoon. The back always is locked. You must be mistaken?"

Mistaken. Maggie remembered the self-doubts of a few days ago. She took a deep breath and with a calm voice said, "No, I am *not* mistaken. There was a man in your gallery. He was not very nice. He left through the rear. And now I am leaving, too."

Maggie hurried back to the photography lab and met Allie just as she was coming out, her arms loaded with packages of proofs. Without a word, Maggie took some of the packages.

After they had dropped them in the car's trunk, Allie asked, "What's up? You look like you've seen a ghost!"

They got in the car and Maggie jammed the white hat down so hard on her head that the little flower nearly fell off. "No, I haven't seen a ghost. I'd almost prefer that to what I did see." She described the incident in the gallery. "*Something* is going on and somehow I seem to be connected to it. It involves Andre and Brigitte Fouchet. What picture? That man certainly could be Middle Eastern. What's more, I'm determined to get to the bottom of this. I'm beginning to feel very angry about the whole thing!" Maggie's voice rose and her face was flushed with determination.

Allie glanced at Maggie. "I couldn't agree more. It's getting serious. I wonder if we should tell the police or something. I'm not sure what we can tell them. So far, as far as we know, there's been no crime. Of course, harassment is a crime. But, aside from the man in the green car, we can't prove anything."

"What shall we do? Is there anything we can do? If we contact someone in authority, who should it be?" Maggie asked, so absorbed in her thinking that she hardly noticed their progress down San Vicente Boulevard. After a silence, "Well, at least the Arabs are back! At least, I assume he was an Arab."

Allie looked at her grimly and nodded. "If there's nothing more you want to do while we're out, let's go home and call Ed. I'd like to know if there've been any new developments about Brigitte Fouchet's disappearance. If she's been found, then this could be a very different thing."

They picked up dry cleaning and groceries on their way. With their arms loaded, they entered the house from the carport. The office door opened with difficulty, as if something were against it. Allie looked at Maggie, raised her eyebrows and pushed harder. "What . . . .?"

The office was a shambles. Piles of papers were lying against the door. Allie's files had been opened and the contents scattered around the room. Her desk and worktable, orderly when they had left, were covered with papers. Drawers were hanging open. They pushed the door open and stepped into the room, silent, faces white with shock. Through the open door they could see into Allie's bedroom. It also was in disarray.

"Do you think it's safe to go in?" a shaky squeak from Maggie.

"I don't know," Allie whispered.

Quietly they backed out of the house. Still whispering, "Let's go next door and call the police."

"Best idea. Much safer. This is too scary!" Allie agreed.

Mrs. Asherman, the neighbor, a stylishly coifed woman in her fifties, was solicitous and alarmed. She gave them tea while they waited for the police to arrive. "You know, I didn't notice anything. Nothing out of the ordinary. I thought you'd been away for a while. I mean, your car was gone for a while. But today I didn't notice anything." She stammered on, "Was anything missing?"

"We didn't go in. We couldn't tell. It was a mess." Allie looked more and more uncomfortable.

Time dragged on, slowly, so slowly that reality seemed to be fading.

Mrs. Asherman offered another pot of tea.

Maggie broke the uncomfortable silence, "Did the police say how long it would be?"

Allie shook her head, "No. They didn't say."

"Well, if anyone had been there, surely they'd be gone by now."

"Yeah. I'm sure there's no one there now. Let's go."

Mrs. Asherman twisted her hands together, "Do you think you should?"

Allie smiled at her neighbor, "Mrs. Asherman, thank you so much for your help. I'm sure it's all right now. The police may be there already. We're going home. Please don't worry." She looked at Maggie. They walked across the street to the guesthouse.

At the door they felt less confidant, but encouraged by each other's presence, they once again entered the office. Nothing had changed. Their packages were where they had dropped them. The place was a mess. Cautiously they walked through the office, into the bedroom. It was in chaos. Downstairs it was the same. Books out of shelves, cabinets opened. The food had been taken out of the refrigerator. Even the deck had not been spared. Plants had been overturned.

They wandered through the house in silence, absently picking up a piece of paper or righting an overturned chair. Finally they looked at each other, faces stony with outrage and anger. "This makes me so mad!" Maggie said through clenched teeth. "Really, really mad! Where are the police? How long ago did we call? This is too much!"

Just then the doorbell rang. Allie and Maggie jumped simultaneously. Cautiously they opened the door to two men.

Hello, I'm Lieutenant Garcia and this Sergeant Jackson. Did you call? I understand you've had some trouble here." Lieutenant Garcia was a short man with thinning hair and shiny brown eyes. Sergeant Jackson was taller and plumper, sandy hair, cut short, freckles. They both wore serious faces.

"We certainly have. Please come in. Sorry I can't offer you a seat." she said waving her arm at the chaos.

"Yeah, we see. Just tell us what happened."

"I wish I could. My mother and I went out to run a few errands. When we returned this is what we found. We called you from a neighbor's, but after a while we decided to come back and look around. That's it, really." Allie said.

"Your name, miss?" Sergeant Jackson was making notes in a spiral notebook. He continued, asking them their names, occupations, Maggie's address in Florida and more information that seemed not particularly relevant to Maggie and Allie.

As they toured the little house, they heard an occasional 'tsk' from Lieutenant Garcia. "They made a real mess! Can you tell if anything's missing?"

"No, of course not." Allie seemed exasperated, "But nothing large or obvious is missing. The TV and DVD player are here. So is my computer, both answering machines, the fax, the copy machine. I have several cameras and they all seem to be here. I don't have a lot of jewelry and only a few good things. But nothing of great monetary value. I can check on those." She rummaged around pulling items out of the debris as she spoke. "There're no drugs on the premises, unless you count aspirin," Allie said anticipating the next question.

"This is how they got in," said Lieutenant Garcia, pointing to scratches around the simple doorknob lock. You know, these things are pretty useless. You really ought to get some good dead bolts at least."

"I guess you're right," said Allie, "but this has been such a quiet neighborhood up to now. I've always felt safe here."

"Yeah, up to now!" Changing the subject, he said, "It doesn't look like vandalism. Nothing's been destroyed and none of the usual things have been taken. Looks like they were looking for something in particular. Any idea what that was?" Lieutenant Garcia asked quietly.

Maggie and Allie looked at one another, "No. No, of course not." Then another look.

"Well," Maggie said, "some strange things have been happening. We were just wondering if we should report them or not." She continued, telling them about the man in the green car in Big Sur and about the latest incident in the art gallery. "We weren't sure that there was anything that the police could do. I mean, no one was hurt and nothing really happened."

"There's something to that, ma'am. It's hard to say if there's any connection to this. Jackson's sent for the forensic team. Doubt we'll get any prints. Looks like a professional job. Please don't touch anything until the fingerprint people finish. D'you plan to stay here tonight?"

Allie looked worried, "We hadn't thought about it. What d' you think, Mom?"

Maggie looked at her watch, "Let's see, it's after five now. I think we can put things in enough order by bedtime so we can sleep. I don't think I'll feel afraid. How about you? We could find a hotel in Santa Monica for the night?"

"Let's play it by ear. I want to get things back to normal as soon as possible. If we feel afraid at bedtime we could run over there. For that matter, we could stay with my friend Eleanor in Pacific Palisades." Allie was beginning to sound more confident.

"Sounds good."

When all the police finally had gone, they started putting the house to rights. Allie worked upstairs and Maggie tackled the downstairs. Physical activity felt good. It helped relieve some of the anger and frustration they both were feeling.

By midnight the house looked much better. The office files would require more attention, but nearly everything else was in place.   "Mom, let's quit for tonight," Allie called.   "Do you want to find a hotel?"

Maggie climbed the stairs and said, "I'm not afraid to stay here if you're not.   Whoever it was, whatever they were doing, if they'd wanted to hurt us they had a perfect opportunity when we first came back and they didn't, so I think it's okay."

"Okay.   We stay here.   Let's get some sleep." Allie pushed a strand of hair out of her eyes.   "Mom?"

Maggie looked at her in response.

"Mom, thanks.   I don't know what I'd have done without you.   This has been pretty scary, and it's really good to have you here.   Thanks."

Maggie turned.   "For whatever I've done, you know you're welcome.   I feel I should be thanking you." A pause. "I love you, Allie."

"I know.   Me, too."

Maggie's body seemed to relax in painful little stages as she lay on the sofa bed.   She hadn't realized how tired she was. In spite of her fatigue or maybe because of it, sleep did not come quickly.   The events of the day flashed through her mind, movies projected on an internal screen.   The cold, foggy morning.   Ed's call.   The news about Brigitte Fouchet.   The incident at the gallery and the break-in here at the house.   This day had seemed at least a week long.   But outside the moon was shining, cool silver rays, and she could hear the waves hitting the beach far below.   Who could have done this to Allie's house? Tomorrow.

Chapter Four

Wednesday dawned with the sun shining weakly through the coastal haze. Maggie opened her eyes and lay quietly for a few moments. She heard soft footsteps and then a quiet whisper, "Mom, are you awake?"

"I am," she said positively, "and what's more I'm up!" She stood up and started putting the sofa into its daytime mode. "How about you? Are you up? How're you feeling? Did you sleep? D'you have plans for today?"

"Wait, hold it! I'm not thinking yet. Give me a few moments," was the sleepy reply.

They dressed quickly and discussed possible plans for the day. The two walked through the house, carrying tea mugs and examining their clean-up efforts of last night.

"Mom, I really need to finish putting the office back together."

"Okay, what can I do to help?"

Maggie sorted papers and photos into related stacks around the floor. Allie inspected and stuck them back in the file cabinets. Sooner than they expected the papers had disappeared into the file cabinets and the clean-up job was officially completed.

"Whew!" Allie breathed a huge sigh of relief. "It's good that most of my negatives are stored at the lab. This could have been a real disaster if they'd been here. Thank you for helping, Mom. I'm relieved to have that done. Now. What next?"

"Well, we can't ignore that something's going on. It looks like we're involved. It all must be connected. I'd like to do something, but for the life of me, I can't think what," Maggie said.

"Neither can I." Allie sat hunched over with her head in her hands. Finally, she straightened and said, "Do you think I should call Ed? Maybe he has some news about the Fouchets or some idea?"

Maggie looked at her, "I don't know. I'm so frustrated and in the dark that I feel like grasping at any straw. We're getting no help from the police. They seemed to want to focus on the break-in only. It's a bit like sitting in a bed of poison ivy and putting calamine on the rash. Calling Ed is your decision."

Allie smiled at Maggie's metaphor, "Well, I'm itching to get to the bottom of it!" Allie straightened her shoulders and said, "We need more information. Things are getting too intense. We could be in real danger. Neither of us is incredibly strong physically. I'm going to call him." She picked up the telephone and punched the numbers.

When Allie had Ed on the line, Maggie rose to walk out to the deck in order to give Allie privacy for the call. But Allie motioned her to stay. "Ed, I'm calling for a couple of reasons. First, the Fouchets. D'you have any news about them? My mom is with me and I'm going to put on the speaker phone."

"Hello, Mrs. McGill." Ed's deep voice boomed into the room. "Things are not good here. Now Andre Fouchet's missing, too. That is, he left his hotel room yesterday afternoon and hasn't returned."

As they listened Allie's face became even more grave. "Whew! Poor Andre and Brigitte. I hope you have good news soon. The second thing I called about is to tell you what happened to Mom and me yesterday. We wonder if it could be connected to what's happening up there." Allie gave him an account of Maggie's gallery adventure and of the break-in, stopping from time to time to consult with Maggie and to clarify when Ed had a question. Finally, she stopped talking. There was a long silence.

"Allie, I don't know what's going on, but I'm glad you called. We need to get to the bottom of it. Everything we learn makes the situation sound more and more ominous. I'm gravely concerned for your and your mother's safety. I'm wondering what we can do to ensure it. What are your plans? Will you be there for a while? I'd like to make some calls. I think the people up here need to hear your story. It is okay for me to tell it?"

Allie glanced at Maggie and said, "We may run out for a little while, but we'll be here most of the time. The machine will be on. And I'll have my cell phone with me." She gave him the number. "Of course. Tell anyone. It's no secret as far as I'm concerned!"

Maggie agreed, "Thank you for being concerned, Ed. It's comforting to know someone is doing something."

Allie turned off the speaker and listened a little longer. Maggie strolled out onto the deck. The sun had burned off the haze and once again it was a beautiful warm-cool day with golden sunshine. Maggie heard Allie murmur a word or two and then put down the receiver.

"What d'you think?" Allie asked as she came out on the deck.

Maggie said, "Well, I don't know what he can do, but for the first time I feel better about the situation. It sounds like Ed plans to do something."

"Yeah. We may complain about men, but they can have their good points." Allie grinned. "It's turned out to be a nice day. How about lunch or a walk on the beach? Or shopping? Or something?"

"They all sound good to me. Let me change. I feel grubby." They changed into clean jeans, shirts and walking shoes and headed the little car down the winding streets.

Allie pulled into a shopping center of small boutiques just off the PCH in Malibu. They lunched under bright umbrellas in the courtyard that contained a children's play yard and fountains surrounded by bright flower borders. The sun was warm. Children laughed in the play yard. People smiled and talked in small groups. Allie's eyes met Maggie's. "This is the way it should be. Nice. Normal. People enjoying themselves. No mystery. No fear. Think we're going to get that back?"

"I certainly plan to," said Maggie. "I can't say I'm very fond of the kind of excitement we've been having."

"I know, Mom. I'm so sorry that your vacation has had all this stuff happening."

"Well, I haven't given my counseling practice a thought for several days. So I guess it really has served as a get-away in that respect," Maggie said ruefully.

"How about a walk on the beach?"

"Great."

They parked beside the highway in front of heavy wooden gates centered in a long, high stucco wall. Allie opened the gates with a key and they entered a spacious low loggia in front of low buildings on either side of the gate. The loggia was floored with red Spanish tiles, the roof supported by heavy wooden posts and beams. The beach side was furnished with heavy wicker chairs and chaises. Pots of scarlet geraniums hung from the beams. Maggie caught her breath, "How lovely," she said. "And how elegant!"

"No big deal, Mom. This is owned by the neighborhood association and is maintained for our use. Isn't it cool?"

They left their shoes on the loggia and walked across the broad beach to the water's edge. Maggie drew a deep breath and exhaled slowly. She turned around in a little circle, taking in the entire scene. To the north the low coastal mountains curved to form the northern edge of the Los Angeles basin. To the south she saw the coastline continue, lined with houses, and farther down, taller buildings. Behind them were the Malibu hills and somewhere Allie's house. Barely discernible across the water was an island that Maggie thought must be Catalina. "This is simply beautiful."

"I know. I come whenever I can. Let's walk." They strode briskly up the nearly deserted beach. Maggie had to scramble to keep up with Allie's long legs. After a while they turned and more slowly started back down the beach. When she had caught her breath, Maggie asked Allie about her conversation with Ed.

"He's just great," said Allie. "You heard most of it. After you stepped out on the deck he said that he really wishes he could go to Vienna and be here, too. Oh, life! He agreed that staying friends is the most important thing. He seems determined to help us get to the bottom of this mystery. You know, Mom, he's a good person."

"I know he must be, honey."

Allie kicked the sand with her bare foot. "Yeah! Well, I guess if this were the love affair of the century, we'd find a way to be together. That we haven't probably says something."

They walked in the bright sunshine in silence for a while. The beach was becoming more populated. Other walkers and runners smiled in greeting as they passed by. Maggie was thinking that the collective physique on this beach was different and much more interesting than that at home in Florida. She watched a figure approaching them. Tall, muscular, bronzed by the sun. He was jogging at the water's edge. In his bright yellow running shorts he easily could have been an advertisement for suntan lotion or body building or vitamins or. . .. He looked at them as he came nearer, smiled, and passed by. Maggie turned to watch him and was embarrassed to find that he had turned around, was running in place and looking back at them. She turned to comment to Allie only to find Allie, also, had twisted around to look back at the runner.

Allie, her face turning red, grinned and said, "He's very attractive, isn't he?"

"Attractive is an understatement. Wow! Quite an eyeful!" Maggie said. "He seemed intrigued by you. For a moment I thought he was going to come back and say something."

"Well, yes. I guess so. I've seen him down here before. He must run a lot. He really is good looking," Allie answered. "I'd like to meet him, but he never stops running. I guess I could throw myself across his path. I wonder if he'd stop or just leap over my inert form and keep on going."

"Well, I think he'll recognize you the next time you meet!" Maggie commented.

Laughing, they continued down the beach, enjoying the hot sun on their faces.

Back at the clubhouse, they lounged in the dark green wicker chairs on the loggia, silently enjoying the sun and the air. Allie closed her eyes. After a while Maggie closed hers too. It was very peaceful, listening to the waves on the beach, the gulls crying.

"Could I have a word with you, Mrs. McGill?" The deep, gruff voice was very close. Maggie and Allie jumped and opened their eyes. His eyes still were tired. The suit still was rumpled. Maggie recognized the man immediately and she was sure that somewhere near there must be a small green car.

"WHO ARE YOU?"

"And what do you want?"

"Why have you been following us?"

The man nodded at Allie and looked at Maggie. "My name is Harry Cavanaugh." He reached in his pocket and brought out a small leather case that he handed to Maggie. "I work for the CIA. I wonder if I could ask you a few questions."

"Oh, my goodness!" Maggie took the ID, glanced at it and handed it to Allie.

Allie examined the ID carefully, "Mr. Cavanaugh, whatever is going on?" She stood up looking serious and severe.

"That's what we'd like to know. We thought you, Mrs. McGill, might know something about an investigation we're working on, but after last night's break-in we're afraid you might be in some danger. I don't want to alarm you, but we don't want either of you hurt."

"How do you know about the break-in? Have the police contacted you?" Allie asked.

"No. We're not working with the police at this time. Our investigation is only that right now. But we've got our sources. What about the break-in? Any idea who did it or why?"

Maggie and Allie stared at him and then looked at each other, bewilderment in their faces. "No, of course not. Nothing was taken that we're aware of. They just made an awful mess. It took us a long time to clean it up." Maggie said indignantly.

"On the airplane, Mrs. McGill, you sat beside a French couple. They were at a party you attended in San Francisco. Did you know these people before the airplane trip?" Cavanaugh stared at the two women intently.

"No. I'd never seen them before the flight. I was amazed when they showed up at the party. I really didn't know what to think," Maggie said cautiously.

Cavanaugh continued his questioning, "Did they say anything out of the ordinary to you? Did they give you anything?"

"They said little I could even understand. If they were trying to give me some sort of message, they or I failed. I don't know French and their English was not that great. The girl spoke very little English at all." Maggie shook her head, "They didn't give me anything. They were young and sweet. Honeymooners. When the movie began I took a nap. That's about all. We said good-bye and left the plane. That was it." Maggie continued, "But you should know. You were right there. You sat just behind us."

"That's true. What you've said bears out what I saw. Except for one thing. Andre Fouchet speaks excellent English. I wonder why he didn't use it that day." Cavanaugh's brow wrinkled as he thought.

"Did you follow us to the lodge in Big Sur?" Maggie asked. Even though her instincts told her he was to be trusted, the events of the last week had left her wary.

Harry Cavanaugh sighed audibly and said, "Yes, I did."

"Why?" From Allie.

"Why? Well, you sat beside them for several hours on the plane. You talked to them. But then, some other people began to show interest in you."

"What!!?"

He looked even more tired. "People who at first seemed to be interested only in Andre Fouchet began to show interest in the two of you. We wondered why. At first we suspected you were working with them, but then we weren't so sure. After the break-in, we became concerned for your safety. We hoped you'd be able to tell us something useful."

Allie raised her eyebrows. "Other people? Showed an interest in us? Who? How? What do you mean?"

"As you know, Andre Fouchet is an expert on Middle Eastern terrorism. He knows more about terrorist tactics, terrorist organizations and the people in them than probably any other man on earth. Fouchet is a very valuable resource for us. By the way, he's not quite as young as he looks."

Allie interrupted, "'As we know?' What do you mean? How would you know what we know about Andre Fouchet?"

Cavanaugh took in a long breath. "You're quick, Miss McGill. I guess I may as well tell you. After your return from San Francisco, we installed electronic listening devices in your apartment and on your phone."

"You what?" Maggie's face was pale with shock and anger. She looked at Allie who was nodding her head slowly.

"It fits together, Mom. The vans in the neighborhood. That feeling of not being quite alone. Didn't you sense that too?" Allie turned to Cavanaugh. "So after hearing our conversations with Ed you could be pretty sure about our level of involvement."

"You understand we had to know how you fit into the whole thing," Cavanaugh said.

"I understand," Maggie said slowly, "and I still can't help feeling violated. It's a terrible invasion of our privacy. I almost feel more violated by knowing this than I did yesterday at the gallery or after the house was broken into." She looked at Cavanaugh. "I can't help it, that's the way I feel."

"I'm sorry about that," Cavanaugh said, looking even more tired. "But it was necessary. What about the gallery? We heard your accounts on the telephone, of course. Is there anything else you can tell us about it? Exactly what did the man look like?"

Maggie frowned as she concentrated, "He was very large, tall, but broad, too. Sort of like a footfall player or a wrestler. And he was dark skinned, Middle Eastern looking, black hair and black eyes. He probably was in his late thirties, but I can't be sure about that. There was a look in his eyes that was memorable; they shone, but, even so, there was a flatness to them, almost a dead look. I don't know. It's hard to describe."

"You said he had an accent?"

"Yes, he had a slight accent. I am guessing Middle Eastern again. He was wearing western clothes. No turbans this time. . .." Maggie stopped. She became very still, her mouth slightly open. It seemed that she had stopped breathing. Slowly she raised her eyes to Allie and Cavanaugh. "You know, I think the man in the gallery may be the guy who was on the flight. He looked different without the turban, but . . .Yes, I think it was the same man." To Cavanaugh, "Do you remember seeing a turbaned man on the flight?"

Cavanaugh smiled. "Oh yes, Mrs. McGill, I remember him. This confirms what we had assumed. Thank you." He stared at the tiled floor for a moment. Peering up under his lashes at Maggie, he asked, "What about the picture? Any idea what that was about?"

Maggie shook her head, "None at all."

"Now, Mr. Cavanaugh, would you answer a few of our questions?" Allie stood straight and tall, her arms crossed.

"Any that I can, Miss McGill," Harry Cavanaugh said with a smile.

"You followed us from San Francisco to Big Sur?"

He nodded.

"Why did you ask for us at the lodge? That seems a strange thing to do."

"Not only strange, it wasn't real smart, er, that is, professional. There were some interesting types staying at that lodge. It was like a parade from San Francisco to Los Angeles. Thanks to you, it was the scenic route. Actually, I was following the car that was following you. I got there just as the No Vacancy sign went up. So I had the pleasure of spending the night in the car." Harry stretched his neck to one side. "Not the most comfortable night I've had. It was damned cold. But I was lucky to get something to eat. I don't think our friends made it to the drive-in in time." He grinned at the memory.

"The green car," murmured Maggie.

Harry continued, "The next morning I couldn't find you two anywhere. Your car was still there. When I found that damned trail I panicked. I started down the trail much too fast and then I saw Ahmed coming up in a hurry. I had a few uneasy moments until I saw a couple farther down on the trail. They were good news for the two of you!"

"Oh dear," Maggie said. "But who is Ahmed?"

Harry Cavanaugh passed his hand over his face as if to brush away the fatigue, "Ahmed is one of the leaders of the group we're checking out. We suspect there's a higher-up. But Ahmed's the closest we've been able to get to the top. The other person has kept a very low profile. We don't know what he. . .hell, we don't even know for sure whether it's a man or a woman. . .. We just know that this top person exists."

Allie sat down in a wicker chair and motioned Cavanaugh to do the same. "But no one followed us when we left the lodge. I made very sure of that."

Cavanaugh sat down and sighed again. "I followed the others but they lost interest in you at that point. We were pretty sure where you were headed and we were very interested to know where they were going. As you may know there's more than one way to keep track of an automobile."

"This is too much! You had one of those things on my car?"

"Yeah, 'fraid so.

"Were you in the big black car?" asked Maggie.

"No, we were tracking it," Cavanaugh said.

"But it went right on by us in Santa Barbara."

"Yeah, we're not sure why they did that. Maybe they spotted us." Cavanaugh sat silent for a moment and then changed the subject. "Anything else we should know?"

Maggie decided she trusted him after all. Eyes don't lie. "Well, if you heard the phone conversations, you have most of the story."

Allie frowned thoughtfully, "Mom, how about the rock in the Tea Garden?

Maggie looked at Allie and then at Cavanaugh, "I thought it was just an accident."

"Tell me what happened and let me decide that," Cavanaugh encouraged.

As Maggie told him about the rock incident, Harry became quieter and more thoughtful. "It's hard to say for sure, of course, but I'm inclined to be suspicious of it. Let us do a little investigation. Did you report it? Did you make an official complaint?"

"No. I thought it was an accident. I wasn't hurt. I didn't want to make a fuss. I'm on vacation after all." Maggie smiled weakly.

"Yeah, vacation. Well, I'll look into it," Cavanaugh said grimly.

"What happens next? What should we do?" Allie asked. "Can you arrest these people?"

"No, we don't have any proof that they've done anything illegal. We suspect there may be bigger things in the works. We want to watch them for a while and see what happens."

"What about the break-in at my house?" Allie asked. "That was illegal."

"Yes, it was. Whoever did it probably was a pretty small fish. We want the big guy. We know there is one. We suspect he or she might be behind the break-in at your house, but that's not the way to find that person," Cavanaugh explained patiently. "I wish we could figure out what they're looking for. That'd be a big help."

"Don't you know? In the gallery he said it was a picture. But for all we know, it could be a work of art or a photo or anything. Believe me, if we had any idea about that we'd let you know," Maggie said.

"Yeah, it's pretty scary knowing there are people out there watching us and wanting something from us and we don't have an idea who they are or what they want or what they may do next," said Allie.

"Yeah, I know how you feel. Well, we'll keep a closer eye on you than before."

"That, I guess, should make us feel safe?" Allie said.

"I hope so. There's another alternative. We could put you up in a safe house. That should be fairly secure."

"What do you mean, 'safe house'?" Allie asked.

"Oh, we've got a house or two, staffed by our people, where folks in trouble can drop out and be protected," Harry answered.

"Safe. Like being in prison. No, thank you." Maggie shuddered at the thought.

"The alternative is a something like being a worm on the end of a line," Allie said, looking at her mother. "The choices aren't that great. Are you sure, Mom, that's the one you want?"

"I think so. Neither alternative would be my first choice. But what about you? How d'you feel? If you opt for the safe house, I'll go along with it. We could catch up on our reading or something." Maggie looked back at Allie.

"I'm with you, Mom. No prisons for me. Scary as it is, I'd rather not be cooped up. Besides, I'm beginning to feel really angry. I'd like to find these guys and . . .. Well, I don't know what, but I'd like to do something!"

They turned to Cavanaugh. He stood up, "I don't know whether you two are very brave or just foolish, but I understand how you feel. We'll do all we can to protect you. As for doing 'something', leave that to us. I'd like you two to continue just as you would if this were not happening. That is, I'd like you to look as normal as possible. Please don't take any unnecessary chances. Stay together. Try not to wander out alone. No more steep mountain trails, please."

"Okay. We'll be careful. How can we contact you if we should need to?" asked Allie.

"We'll be close by. I'll give you a number. Use it only if you have to. It's a direct line. Ask for Harry. Give your name and location. I'll get back to you. I want both of you to memorize this number, don't write it down. Now repeat it after me, 213-555-6366."

Dutifully the two women repeated the number several times.

Maggie nodded, "We've got it."

"I must go. I have been here too long already. By the way, the green car's gone. I got something less noticeable and considerably faster. Wait here a few minutes and then just do whatever you'd normally do." With that Harry Cavanaugh walked quickly along the loggia and down the beach a few houses before he disappeared behind one of them.

Allie raised her eyebrows and gave a long, low whistle, "Wow! Shades of James Bond!"

Maggie laughed. "Some James Bond! I don't know when I've seen a more nondescript, innocuous appearing person." She thought for a moment. "But maybe that's as it should be. He did seem to know what he was doing. At least, I certainly hope so. Do you feel frightened, Allie?"

"Not now. Just sort of excited. It's getting real interesting. At least some of the mystery is solved."

"Ditto," Maggie said vehemently.

"Do you think we've waited long enough? Let's go." Allie got up and moved toward the large wooden doors.

In the car Allie said, "That'll be a hard act to follow. But is there anything special you'd like to do now?"

Maggie grinned at her and glanced in the side mirror as they pulled onto the highway. She watched Allie also checking the mirrors. "I wonder if I'll ever be in a car again without checking the mirrors. Well, I don't care what we do next. Something peaceful and unexciting, please. Is there anything you need to do?"

"Not really. The photography business is caught up right now. Friday I'll need to pick up some prints and send them out, but right now nothing is pressing." Allie found an opening in the heavy traffic and the little car shot ahead.

Again each of them checked the rearview mirrors. "If anyone is following us I don't see them," Maggie said. "I keep thinking about our conversations at your house. I wish I could remember all we said. Even though I accept their reasons for bugging it, I can't help feeling violated. Do you feel that too?"

"You bet I do. I don't even want to go home. That's a weird feeling! My house has been such a haven for me. It doesn't feel safe or comfortable anymore." Allie's voice sounded small and defenseless.

At last they decided on a movie and dinner before going home. The movie was light and funny. They lingered over dinner. Finally, when they could put it off no longer they headed back up the PCH, the car growled up the winding streets and they were home. They passed a utility company van. "Versatile, but hardly creative!"

On the deck they sipped tea and watched the last of the sunset's red glow fade from the sky. As they watched, the ocean changed from burnished gold to deep red to black. Below them lights came on and sparkled in the night. There seemed to be little more to say. Anyway, it made one self-conscious knowing that some unknown person could hear one's every word. So, after double-checking doors and windows, hot showers and bed.

Under the down comforter, Maggie thought about the day. She thought this certainly was the most exciting vacation she'd ever had. She wondered about tomorrow; prayed for their safety, for the safety of Andre and Brigitte, and finally gave begrudging thanks for the protection of Harry Cavanaugh and his organization. She heard Allie's voice from upstairs, "We're going to be okay, Mom."

"Yes, I know," she answered. *At least I hope so.*

Chapter Five

Raucous whistling and singing. Maggie opened her eyes to bright sunlight streaming in through the leafy canopy. Above the house the occupants of the canopy were in riotous voice, apparently filled with joy, welcoming the beautiful day. Maggie groaned and covered her head with the pillow. Morning was happening much too soon. Then, with a rush, the memories of yesterday's events returned and made more sleep impossible. Quietly she rose and folded up the sofa bed.

When Allie stumbled down the stairs an hour later, Maggie, wrapped in a heavy robe, was sipping tea. "G'morning, Mom. You're up early. What's up?"

"Good morning, Honey. Did you sleep well?"

"Better than I had expected. Amazing."

"Me, too. At least until your tree dwellers decided to greet the morning." Maggie grinned at her. "As soon as you're awake, how about a walk before breakfast?" Maggie waved her arm indicating unseen listening ears.

Allie's eyes widened and she said, "Sounds good." Quickly they slipped into jeans, sweaters and walking shoes.

It was a spectacular morning. The early sun slanting behind them highlighted the tops of the trees below leaving many of the streets still in shadow. Far below, a low-lying mist, resting on the water, was dissolving before their eyes. It seemed as if every bird in Los Angeles County had decided to congregate in the Malibu hills and burst into song.

"Wow! This is worth the trip, even if we didn't need our privacy," Allie exclaimed.

Maggie sighed with pleasure. "That's so. I wanted to get away from the house so we could talk. That *thing* is so inhibiting. Now it seems a shame to talk about anything other than this marvelous morning."

Allie nodded her agreement. "Heavenly. Thank you or thank the situation for getting us up and out here. What's up? What'd you want to talk about?"

Maggie sat down on a rock and stared out at the Pacific. "Well, this situation. I mean, here we are, our lives are in a sort of limbo. With so much on our minds, work doesn't seem possible and with the big EAR in the house and on the phone, just visiting is a drag. With the threat of we don't know what, even having fun doesn't work. I feel completely frustrated. How about you?"

Allie looked at her mother with a combination of surprise and amusement. "Mom, I agree. Our hands seem to be tied. Miserable feeling, isn't it!"

Maggie nodded. "It comes down to a matter of control and power. We're feeling powerless, out of control, because we can't think of any appropriate action, even a meaningless one. It's no fun."

Allie looked thoughtful and said, "Yes. But do we have a choice?"

"I agree. It's scary. Apparently there's a lot more to this than we know. We do know, however, that the Fouchets are missing. We know that we've been threatened and frightened. We know that our lives are being upset in ways that we don't deserve. It makes me very angry." Maggie stopped for a moment, then continued, "No, not angry. It makes me furious!"

Allie grinned for a moment at her mother's fierceness. "Yeah, me too. Well, what're our options? Do we have any? At this point, apparently we've been targeted by some middle-eastern group, the CIA is monitoring our every word and move, and we don't know what's behind it all." She sat on a neighboring rock and sighed.

"True. What else is true is that we don't care for our options. But are there any other choices?" Maggie glanced at her daughter.

Allie picked up a stick and doodled in the loose soil at her feet. "Well, let's see." She made a "1" in the dirt and jabbed a period beside it. Then she wrote, "CIA safe house."

"That's choice number one."

Maggie added, "Choice number two is stay at home with surveillance."

Allie wrote, "2. Home."

"Both are pretty passive choices. I wish we could find a constructive course of action that would end the mystery and let us get on with our visit." Allie wrote a "3." in the dirt and looked inquiringly at Maggie.

Maggie took a deep breath and said, "Of course, we don't want to put ourselves in any more danger. I've certainly had as much of that kind of excitement as I want. Do you think our problems are connected to the Fouchets' disappearance?"

"It certainly seems so." Allie's head jerked up and she drew a quick breath. "I just remembered. Ed promised to call yesterday. I wonder what's happening up there. For all we know the Fouchets could have been found and the mystery could be over."

Maggie said, "You're right." She hunched over, doodling flowers and shapes in the loose dirt. "We could just run away for a while. You know, go to the mountains or something until this situation is cleared up."

Allie looked up in surprise, "D'you want to do that?"

"Not really. But it's an option. We need to consider every one."

Allie frowned, "Yeah, you're right." She wrote a "3" in the sand. "Well, that's not exactly a complete plan, but it's something we could do."

They talked until the sun was high in the sky and their stomachs were growling. The dirt in front of the rocks had been marked and wiped out many times. Finally the list was:

Options	Plan
1. CIA safe house	1. Call Ed
2. Home	a. find out about
3. Run away	Fouchets
4. Investigate	b. find out about Arabs

They agreed that the first three options were unsatisfactory. The problem was that they didn't know how to begin their investigation beyond making the phone call.

Allie said, "Who knows! When we talk to Ed we may find out something that'll give us a lead. All we need is a handle. Something to work on." Then changing the subject, "Mom, I'm starving. Let's go while we still have the strength to get down off this hill! I need to pick up my mail and we can have brunch or something at Brandon's. We can call from there."

Brandon's was bright, airy and casual, open early for breakfast and late for snacks. The cuisine was pure Californian, fresh, creative and delicious. Allie assured her mother that movie stars could be seen there, but Maggie had yet to see one. Still wearing their faded jeans and sweaters, they wolfed down eggs and potatoes and many cups of tea.

After they collected Allie's mail, Maggie asked, "What about Ed?"

Allie wrinkled her brow, "For some reason I'm a little reluctant to call. After all, he hasn't called me. It doesn't seem quite right somehow to tell him about Harry Cavanaugh. I can't say why."

"I know what you mean," her mother said, understanding Allie's confusion.

"Maybe I could call Ed and not tell him about Harry. What d'you think?"

In response Maggie picked up the telephone and handed it Allie. Allie punched in the numbers. "Hello, Ed. Yes, we're fine." She listened intently as the deep voice rumbled on. A truck roared by on the PCH. More voice rumbles. Then, "Oh, we're out running errands". More rumbles. "Impulse, I guess. We've been concerned about the Fouchets." The call continued for a few more minutes. Then good-byes and Allie hung up.

Allie looked uncomfortable, "I really didn't like that. I guess I'm not cut out for deception. Anyway, he had no news. I'm afraid we're at an impasse."

"Maybe we should take Harry up on his offer. Or maybe we should try to forget the whole problem." As she said it Maggie knew how silly the last suggestion was.

"Oh, I don't know, Mom. It seems as if we're going in circles. Maybe we should disappear for a while. I hate the idea of giving up, but I can't think of another rock to turn over."

Maggie gazed at her for a moment. She looked around, first at the trendy shopping center, then across the highway at the sun-dappled hills, the university buildings in the distance. "Me, neither. Maybe we should follow Harry's advice and carry on as usual. It's a lovely day." Maggie took a deep breath. She brightened and said, "I know. Let's look at those condos you mentioned. I'd love to see them. It might be fun."

"Okay. We could do that." Allie straightened up a little. "In fact, that might be a perfect thing to do. Let's go. They're just down the road."

Maggie pulled her camera out of her purse and said, "Good. I'm going to drop that roll of film for developing then I'm ready." She entered the drug store and returned a few moments later, stuffing candy bars into her purse. "Ready! How about some chocolate? It's my favorite antidote to frustration."

The condos were tiered up the hillside like a huge misshapen wedding cake, pale peachy pink and vaguely reminiscent of Roman and Grecian architecture. A tastefully discreet sign directed them to a sales office where they were greeted as potential buyers, and then directed to the next floor to tour nine different models. Armed with pamphlets and price lists, Allie and Maggie ascended to the third floor and started their tour. The model condos were scattered along the second and third floors of the building. Each model was designated by a small plaque indicating its model name and number. The apartments were spacious and airy and beautifully decorated. Having the place to themselves, Allie and Maggie wandered from apartment to apartment, exclaiming about one feature and another. "Allie, look at this deck. It has a marvelous view of the ocean."

Allie twirled around in a huge closet. "These walk-in closets are heavenly! What fun!"

They entered another apartment. "Look, Allie, there's a downstairs in this one." Maggie bounced down the stairs while Allie examined the kitchen. Maggie wandered through a game room into a laundry room. She reached for a door, wondering where it might lead. Suddenly, steel arms closed around her from behind. A heavy hand clamped fabric against her month and nose, a sickly sweet smell. Maggie tried to twist away. She tried to scream. She was aware of a small whimper coming from somewhere and then darkness descended. She was enveloped in deep black velvet, spinning down, down, down.

The two men looked at each other. Holding Maggie's motionless body in his arms, the bulky swarthy man said, "At last. Look in her purse. Is it there?"

The smaller man shook is head as he dumped the contents of her purse on the floor.

"Hurry. The other one will be here in a minute."

The small man gathered the spilled contents back into the purse. Together they carried Maggie through the door, outside, along the base of the apartments to a construction parking lot where they put her into the back seat of a long black automobile. The whole operation took only a few moments.

The large man slipped through the laundry room door just as Allie entered the laundry room, calling, "Mom? Where have you gotten to? Come see the kitchen up . . .." She broke off as she saw the tall dark man. "Who are you? Have you seen my mother?"

"Yes, Miss McGill. Come. No one hurt." He held a particularly ugly looking gun close to his side. He spoke in heavily accented English.

Allie gasped. "Where's my mother? What've you done? What do you want? Who are you?"

"No talking. Come. No questions. I take you to mother. Come now. Quiet." He gestured with the gun, a small inconspicuous gesture that took on enormous proportions to Allie's wide eyes.

With shaking knees Allie walked through the outside door. The man walked close behind her. She could feel the barrel of the gun just touching her ribs from the back. The back door of the long black car opened, a hand shoved from behind and she found herself sprawled across the top of her mother's inert body.

"Oh, my God." Allie gasped. Then shaking her mother, "Mom, Mom, are you okay?" Allie's voice rose in alarm. Maggie's body was as limp as a rag doll. Allie could get no response at all from her. She took her mother's wrist and was reassured to find a strong, steady pulse. "Oh, what have they done? The bastards!" Tears fell down her cheeks. Then she sniffed the remnants of the heavy sweet smell. They must have drugged her.

Through the heavily tinted windows Allie saw that the car was moving rapidly along the PCH. Familiar sights looked both strangely unfamiliar and poignantly familiar at the same time, as if she were watching a film of a long ago, happier time. As she watched, dark covers slid over the windows, apparently controlled from the front. A heavy black partition separated her from the front seat and the two men. In the dark Allie explored the surfaces of the doors. She did not really expect to find a handle and she did not. As well as she could, Allie stretched her mother out along the wide back seat, with her head in Allie's lap.

She focused on the movement of the car, attempting to count stops and turns, hoping to figure out where they were heading. The car was well insulated and the outside noises were muffled. Even so, Allie felt sure they had turned away from the ocean and that they were traveling through heavy traffic. After about an hour the car slowed and started climbing, making several sharp turns. Finally it eased slowly to a stop. She could hear muffled voices and a mechanical sound, maybe a garage door closing. The car door opened to a dim light.

The large dark man grunted, "Out."

Squinting in the light, Allie hesitated, "What about my mother?"

He said again, "Out." He grabbed Allie by the arm and jerked her from the car. Maggie's head bounced against the seat as Allie's lap disappeared.

Standing beside the car, Allie looked around at the interior of a roomy four-car garage. On the far side of the garage was a bright red Ferrari. Otherwise the garage seemed austerely clean. No miscellaneous stuff. Allie wrinkled her nose. There was a scent of fresh masonry. She felt a nudge in her ribs and looked around straight into flat black eyes. Behind the eyes was a small dark man, thin, greasy, black hair, a narrow ferret sort of face with a scraggly black mustache.

In heavily accented English he said, "Go. This way." He indicated that she head for a door in the corner of the garage. Together they walked into a spacious, sparsely furnished house. Allie stumbled in the dim light. A hand shoved her into an elevator. Up. The hand pushed her down a long hall and into a bedroom that was paneled in mirrors. She had time to notice an enormous bed, night stands, two deep armchairs and an opening

that probably led to a dressing room and bath. The smaller of
the two men indicated that she lie down on the bed. With a
shiver she did so. He produced a rope and tied her feet and
hands. Allie tested her bonds, but was hardly able to move a
finger.

In a few moments the large dark man arrived carrying her
mother in his arms. He placed her on the opposite side of the
bed, walked out and closed the door. The room was in total
darkness. Allie closed her eyes and talked to the darkness,
calling on every resource inside and outside of herself she could
think of.

"Harry? Pete here. We lost them."

"What?. . . When?. . . Where?. . . How?. . . Tell me
you're joking!"

"No, really. They were just fine. They went for a walk this
morning. Those are the walkingest women I've ever seen! I'm
getting in better shape than I ever wanted to be. Then they went
out the road, had breakfast, and made some phone calls. From
there they went out to Malibu Manor, you know, those new
condos out the road. They went in and didn't come out. The
car still is out front. According to the people in the sales office
they were looking at the models. But they are gone. Into thin
air! Poof!"

"Any idea who they called?" Harry asked.

"Nope. But it was long distance. She punched a lot of
buttons."

"Okay, Pete. I want you to go back. Go through every one
of those models. Check out every inch, *every inch.* Check
around outside. Are there people living there?"

"Yeah. They have about forty percent occupancy."

"Good. Talk to everyone there. You know what to do. Do it!"

Harry put down the phone. "Damn!" In his mind's eye he saw the McGill women. Maggie's face floated past, smiling her thanks on the airplane. He saw them happy and laughing in those ridiculous hats on top of the hill in San Francisco. He saw them lounging on the loggia at the Beach Club, Maggie's serious face, Allie's fierce one. "Damn it!"

Chapter Six

Floating up, up. Floating through black water, soft black water. Up. Pain. A heavy, fuzzy feeling in her head. A weird taste in her mouth. Maggie thought it would be nice to brush her teeth. But that would mean moving. She thought about moving for a while. Her left leg and arm were asleep. Shhh! she thought. Mustn't wake them! Her grandmother's joke. She thought about smiling. Too much effort. No sound. But, of course, no sound under water. She thought about opening her eyes. They felt heavy, weighted, glued together. Then she felt herself once again slip down, down into the heavy, black water.

Whispering, mumbling. Didn't they know she needed her rest? The mumbling stopped and Maggie heard a sigh. Her left side was asleep. Maggie thought again about moving. Too heavy. Maybe if she opened her eyes. Heavy. With extraordinary effort she opened one eye. Nothing. Then the other eye. I've gone blind! For the first time she wondered where she was. She shifted her eyes. They seemed to be the only part of her that was mobile. Blackness. Then in the blackness, tiny sparkles of light. "Stars," she squeaked softly.

"Mom! Mom, are you all right? Oh, Mom. Oh, Mom. Thank God! You're awake!" Allie said breathlessly.

Maggie croaked, "Allie? Allie? Where are you? Do you see the stars?"

Allie said, "They aren't stars. It's just little pieces of light. Reflections in mirrors, I think."

Slowly, with great effort, Maggie turned from her side onto her back. "My goodness, they're everywhere!" she whispered. The electric prickles shot up and down her arm and leg. "Ooooh." Then the memory of the condo and the sweet smelling cloth came back in a flood. "Allie, that nasty man! That nasty cloth! Where are we?"

"I'm not sure. In a house somewhere. Are you okay? Does anything hurt?"

"My head aches a little, but my side was asleep. It's waking up. Ouch!" Then, "Where are you?"

"Here. On the other side of the bed. I'm tied up. Do you think you could untie me?" Allie whispered.

"I'll try. Why are we whispering?"

"Well, I don't know, but they may still be here. We don't want to attract any more attention."

Moving carefully, Maggie stretched and tested her extremities. They seemed stiff and a little sore, but they began to feel more as if they might belong to her. As she tested them, they once again became obedient to her wishes and slowly she rolled over. On her hands and knees she inched forward in the direction of Allie's voice, groping in the dark for Allie. "My goodness, this must be a big bed," she whispered. Then her hand touched Allie. They both sighed, "Whew!"

Maggie found the ropes binding Allie's hands. They were stiff and the knots had been expertly tied. However, after a while Maggie began to loosen the knots. "At last, I think I'm making some headway," she said. "It's hard in the dark."

"Shhh!" From Allie. "Shhh. Don't move! Listen!" Faintly from somewhere they could hear muffled voices that seemed to be coming nearer. "Quick, Mom. Lie down again. Pretend to be out still."

Maggie scrambled across the bed, lay on her left side once again and attempted to quiet her breathing. A door opened. A rough, masculine voice, "No. Everything's okay. Old woman still out. They not go anywhere." The door closed. A key turned the lock.

Sighs. "That was scary. Good ears, Allie." Maggie rolled over and once again started working on the ropes. As she worked, she mumbled indignantly to herself, "Old woman! Really!" Slowly, slowly first one loop and then another. As her bonds began to loosen, Allie wiggled her fingers and wrists. "Hold still. I'm not finished yet." Then, at last Allie's hands were free. They both rubbed and flexed her hands and fingers, helping the circulation to return. Together they worked on her feet.

When Allie's feet were free and working again the two women started to explore. Cautiously they crawled off the bed and worked their way to the perimeter of the room. Slowly they felt their way around it. The walls, they found, were hard and slick—glass, mirrors. Then they turned a corner and found an opening. Maggie pulled a slat away and a shaft of slanting moonlight came into the room. One wall of the room was glass covered by shiny vertical blinds. "They must be chrome," Maggie whispered. Blinking, they poked their faces through the blinds and gasped in unison. They could see the Los Angeles basin spread out below them, sparkling lights as far as they could see.

"We must be somewhere above Hollywood," Allie hissed.

They turned around, holding the slats aside. The ambient light showed them a large bedroom whose walls and ceiling were covered in mirrors. "Wow!" Any small point of light was reflected again and again, creating multiple pinpoints of light— Maggie's stars. "Wow!"

Beyond the glass was a small balcony. Even though it was high above the ground, they tried to open the heavy glass doors. The doors would not budge. "Darn!"

"Now what?"

"We have to get out of here, of course." Allie's voice contained bravado she really did not feel.

Once more, this time standing upright, they inched around the perimeter of the room, past the door. No point trying the knob. Along the wall opposite the bed, to the opening that indeed led to a dressing room, a huge empty closet and a bathroom. "A loo! Thank God! I was beginning to be really nervous. I really need to use this."

"Me too. You first. I'll wait outside. DON'T flush."

"Okay. Next. I'll wait for you. DON'T flush!" They giggled softly.

"That's better! First things first! Now. Let's figure out how to blow this place!" Together they inched around the rest of the room, ending back at the bed.

"Harry?"

"Yeah. Find anything?"

"Not much. But something. One of those condos had a back door that opened out near the construction parking lot. We found a lipstick on the floor near that door. Pale pink. One of the neighbors said she saw a long black car out there this afternoon."

Harry sighed. "That's not much, but it's something. Anything more about the car?"

"Nope."

"It doesn't really matter. We're pretty sure who it was."

Maggie and Allie sat side by side on the edge of the bed. "If this were the movies we'd pull out a hairpin, work some mechanical magic and escape," Allie said dejectedly. "Women don't use hairpins much these days."

Maggie mused, "What do we have to work with? A bed with bed linens. Two night stands with lamps. Two really heavy chairs. A room lined with mirrors—even the ceiling! My God, it makes you think!" She broke into a soft chuckle.

"Mom, back to business. We can analyze the owner later."

"Okay. Okay. I read a novel once where the prisoners wired the doorknob so that when the villains opened the door they were electrocuted. What do you think? We could use the lamp cord." Maggie whispered hopefully.

"Great. But what if we screw it up and electrocute ourselves?"

"What if we don't?" Maggie responded.

"You sound just like Pooh!"

"I know." Maggie grinned in the dark. "But Pooh never let himself feel scared."

Allie whispered, "Yeah. I guess we can use some of that. Okay. Let's check out a lamp. This would be easier if we could see."

"But then they might know we're up and about."

"Yeah, I know." Allie picked up the nearest lamp and followed its cord to the socket. She unplugged it and lifted the lamp. "Ugh. This sucker is *heavy*. Let's see if we can find an outlet near the door." They crawled again examining by touch the walls on either side of the door.

"Psst. Found one. Bring the lamp." Maggie held the cord near the outlet while Allie carried the lamp toward the door, stretching the cord out.

"Rats." The cord was at least eighteen inches too short to reach.

"Now what?"

Maggie sighed and took another deep breath. "Well, Sweetie, I have only one other thought right now. I really liked the electrocution idea. It had so much style!"

Allie whispered impatiently, "Who cares about style. What's the idea? We just need to get out of here."

"We could push the chairs behind the door and bash them with a lamp when they come through the door. No style at all, but probably effective," Maggie said glumly.

Allie smiled. "Sounds perfect to me, Mom. Let's do it!"

With much quiet grunting and panting they pushed the two chairs across the deep carpet to the door and placed one on either side of it. They placed the bed pillows lengthwise on the bed to give what they hoped would give a momentary impression of their two bodies still incapacitated. Finally they each took a heavy lamp and climbed onto a chair to wait.

"If there are two of them, I'll take the first one. You get the second. Okay?" Allie asked.

"Right. You get the first. I'll get the second. Boy, I sure wish I knew karate or something," Maggie whispered.

"Never mind. If we connect with these lamps, that should do it," Allie said with determination.

It seemed as if they waited for hours. They slumped against their respective walls. Maggie wondered if it still was night. Could they have stood on these chairs all night?

"Psst." An urgent hiss from Allie brought Maggie wide awake and alert. Allie's sharp ears had picked up the faint sounds before Maggie heard them. Muffled voices were approaching. Maggie's heart beat faster. She straightened on the chair. Her hands felt suddenly moist and clammy. The key turned in the lock and the door opened. The tall swarthy man entered the room, glanced up at Maggie in shock, then crash! Allie brought the heavy lamp down on his head with all her strength. His shocked face sank from Maggie's sight to be replaced by a small, ferret-like face. Just as the little man turned to run the other way, Maggie brought her lamp down on him. He crumpled without a sound.

"Jeez, Mom. I was afraid for a moment you weren't going to get him! Good job!"

Maggie grinned triumphantly, "Good for you, too. Good for us! Crude, but effective. These two are cluttering up things. Let's pull them inside and tie them up."

They jerked the lamp cords out and tied their captors hands.

"Oh, come on. Let's just get out of here. There were cars in the garage. Let's find some keys." Hurriedly they went through the pockets of the two men. No keys.

"Now why don't they have the keys? Let's search." Quietly and quickly they ran through the house, looking for car keys. It appeared that no one else was there. They ran from the bedroom into a hall, poking their heads into bedroom after bedroom. The rooms were completely bare and empty. One door opened out onto a roof garden that had an even more spectacular view than the bedroom. Back into the house, down stairs. A large empty living room, a small terrace, a lap pool.

"Nice. Come on." Maggie was beginning to feel frantic.

Down more stairs. How many levels? Five or six. Maggie lost count. Finally, in the kitchen, on the counter were keys. Allie grabbed them all. Down another level. At last, the garage. It was as Allie remembered.

"Quick, Mom. Check keys and gas gauges."

Maggie ran to the Ferrari. Quickly she found the ignition key. "This one has a full tank."

"Great. Wait a moment." Allie released the hood on the large black car. She reached inside and pulled the wires from the distributor cap. "Let me drive," Allie called. Maggie already was in the passenger seat. Allie pushed the lighted garage door opener switch, threw the wires into the back of the shiny, red car, jumped into the driver's seat, and started the engine. As the door opened, they eased out into the night. They were in a neighborhood of large houses perched one above the other on tiny lots. Allie pointed the car downhill. They raced away, elated to be free.

Maggie looked over her shoulder at their prison. It was an enormous, multi-leveled white house that appeared still to be under construction. For the first time, Maggie checked her watch. After two. No wonder traffic was so light.

"Mom, I know about where we are. Do you remember the phone number Harry Cavanaugh gave us? I think this might be a good time to use it. See if that phone works." Allie was driving rapidly, taking curves at breakneck speed, doing her best to put the most distance possible between them and the big white house.

Maggie had not noticed the phone perched near her knees. Now she picked it up, held it to her ear. Nothing. She pressed some buttons. Listened again. A dial tone. God bless technology! She took a breath and punched the numbers in.

After one ring, "Hello."

Only one word spoken in a quiet, tired sounding voice, but it sounded heavenly. A whole muscle family in her back and neck relaxed. "Hello, is this Harry?"

"Mrs. McGill? Is that you? My God, we've been worried. Where are you?" The relief was evident in his voice.

"To tell the truth, I'm not exactly sure. We have stolen a car and we're going fast. But I think we are somewhere in Hollywood and moving very quickly away from it."

This somewhat incoherent reply caused Harry to smile his first real smile of the day. He could hear motor and traffic sounds in the background.

"Tell Harry we are heading straight for the Hollywood Freeway. I want to put as much distance as possible between us and this neighborhood as quickly as possible. Describe our car to him. Ask for advice." Allie spoke rapidly and jerkily between fast turns and screeching stops at red lights. The red car alternately roared and growled as Allie worked the gears.

Maggie repeated this information to Harry, giving him street names as she glimpsed them. "We are in a red Ferrari, top down." She gasped as they narrowly missed a convertible that pulled out directly in front of them. The two couples were laughing and seemed not to realize their narrow escape.

"Tell Allie to take it easy," Harry said. "We'll get you an escort as soon as possible. We want you both in one piece," he continued with a chuckle. "Where've you two been? We have been worried about you."

Into the phone she said, "I'm not sure where, Harry. In a big white house up on the hill behind us." Then in an outraged voice, "They kidnapped us!"

The powerful red car zoomed through the quiet streets heading steadily downhill toward the Hollywood Freeway. Street lights, neon signs flashed by dizzily. Maggie was grateful for her seat belt and especially grateful for Allie's skillful driving.

"Another time I might enjoy this," Allie said. "This is some car. It'd be fun to open it up and see what it can do." They bounced through an intersection. Ahead Maggie could see an overpass.

"There! There it is, I think, "Allie said breathlessly. Now, if we can just find an on-ramp. The little car skidded around a corner and accelerated, searching for the entrance to the freeway. "Okay. Here we go. Tell Harry we're. . .. Oh! Oh!!!"

Allie slammed on the brakes and the car skidded to a stop inches from the front fender of a large black car that was blocking their entrance onto the freeway. Allie jammed into reverse gear, spun the car around and headed back onto the streets of Hollywood. The black car followed closely behind them.

"Oh, dear!" Maggie groaned.

"What just happened?" yelled Harry.

Into the telephone she told Harry what had happened.

"Damn!" said Harry.

"Right." Maggie gasped.

"Tell Allie to open that thing up. Tell her to get on the Hollywood heading north if she can. We have two cars up there heading your way!" Harry shouted.

"Get on the Hollywood heading north. Harry has help coming there." Maggie shouted to Allie.

"I'm trying, I'm trying," Allie answered.

"Tell him we're headed west on Franklin. No, we just turned north on Highland. We'll get on it there."

Maggie relayed the message, clutching the telephone like a lifeline.

The little car swung sharply to the left and there was the ramp. They zoomed up the ramp, the heavy black car close behind. Then suddenly Allie jammed on the brakes again. A second black car sat across the ramp. The red car skidded to a stop inches from it. The pursuing black car skidded sideways next to the red car.

"Harry! Oh, my God! Harry. We're surrounded. There are two cars. There are men coming. Oh, dear! Oh, dear! I'm afraid they have us. We were almost . . ." Maggie's voice squealed to a stop as one of the men grabbed the phone from her hand.

"Hello, Maggie, Maggie!!" Harry Cavanaugh called helplessly as a dial tone answered him. He grabbed a second telephone and shouted into it. "They got them! My God! How'd they find them so fast? They're at the Highland ramp onto the Hollywood. Get over there pronto. Maybe you can catch them!" He replaced the phone and groaned in frustration.

Chapter Seven

Allie and Maggie once again were in the back seat of the large black car. "Oh, Mom. I'm so sorry. I really thought we'd gotten away. How do you suppose they found us so quickly?" Allie asked dejectedly.

"I can't imagine unless they had one of those little things on their own car," Maggie answered.

"Rats! I didn't even think of that. That must be it, of course. So it was pretty simple for them. Rats!"

The back seat of the heavy car swung this way and that so that Maggie and Allie clung to each other for support. The car slowed and again they heard the sound of a garage door opening. The car entered and stopped. The door to the back seat opened and two bearded men wearing turbans pulled them from the car. It was the same garage. The disabled black car stood on their left, its raised hood telling a story. Maggie thought they must buy those black cars by the dozen. As they were being led into the house, the far garage door opened and the red car entered.

"You two. . .cause. . .much trouble," one of the men said in heavily accented English. "We fix. . .soon. . .you trouble no more. Me. . .I want fix now." The menace and the threat were blatant.

Maggie was grateful he wasn't making the decisions, because he was a nasty looking character. She imagined that his name might be Bruno. She turned bewildered eyes to her daughter's pale face. Allie attempted a smile of encouragement, but it was more of a grimace.

Instead of being taken upstairs to the bedroom, they were led into an open courtyard and down a few steps to a door in a blank stucco wall. One of the men unlocked the door with a key, opened it and pushed the two women inside.

Maggie and Allie fell on the floor together. "Mom, are you okay?"

"I'm not hurt, but I'm certainly not okay!" Maggie said with some asperity. "How about you?"

"Ditto!" Allie mumbled.

They sat up and looked around. Once again they found themselves in darkness. High on one wall was a small oblong of slightly lighter darkness that probably was a small window. Apparently they were locked in some sort of a storage or garden shed.

"Well, what do you say? Shall we do a Braille explore again? We're getting pretty good at it by now. I wish I had eaten more carrots. Isn't that supposed to give one better night vision?"

"Actually, I don't think diet can make a significant improvement in night vision." The voice was softly melodious, accented and definitely masculine.

"What. . .?"

"Who. . .?"

Maggie and Allie clutched one another and scooted back away from the voice.

The soft masculine voice said, "Please do not be alarmed. I assure you I mean you no harm. It seems that we find ourselves imprisoned by the same people. Therefore, it would seem that we may have a common interest."

"Who . . .who are you?" Allie asked in a small shaky voice.

"Allow me to introduce myself. My name is Mohammed Hadi El Kabir. But, please call me Hadi. It is my favorite of all my names and it also is the most appropriate. May I inquire the names of my most charming fellow prisoners." His vaguely mysterious voice was gentle, with a soft sing-song cadence.

"My name is Allison Lynn McGill and this is my mother, Margaret Ann McGill. You may call me Allie," Allie said.

"How do you do, Hadi. You may call me Maggie," Maggie said.

"How do you do, Allie and Maggie," Hadi said courteously. "Well, how do you suppose it is that Allah has chosen to have us meet in these peculiar circumstances? How is it that you two lovely ladies have attracted the attention of our captors?"

"Well, you see, that's just it," said Maggie. "We haven't the least idea. I came here to visit my daughter. We have done nothing out of the ordinary. But from the beginning of this trip, there have been extraordinary occurrences. It still is very mysterious." Her voice tremulous.

"Tell me exactly what has happened. Maybe I can enlighten you," Hadi said soothingly.

Together Maggie and Allie once again recited the events of the past week, their voices telling their fear and outrage and bewilderment. By silent agreement they omitted reference to their beach club meeting with Harry Cavanaugh.

Hadi listened without interrupting except now and then with a quiet question for clarification. When they had finished he was silent for a few moments. Then he said, "It would seem that there is something that you know or have that you do not know you know or have. Therefore, if we could determine what that something is we might plan a correct course of action."

"A *correct* course of action! The only course of action I'm interested in is getting as far away from this place, this situation and these people as I possibly can, as soon as I can!" Allie's voice conveyed all the frustration and indignation that the events of the last week had brought about.

"Amen. Me, too," said Maggie. "But what about you? Why are you here?"

Hadi murmured musically, "Why am I here? Ah. That is a most interesting question. One with that we could occupy ourselves for years. Why is the moon in the sky?"

"A philosopher! We are caged with a philosopher!" Allie said in disgust.

"Oh, no. I am not a philosopher. I am only a humble servant of Allah," Hadi said.

"Well, humble servant. What about it? Is there a way out of this place?" asked Maggie.

Hadi said, "Now we come back to the correct course of action. There are times, you know, when the correct course is inaction. We must first determine what the proper course is in this situation."

A duet of disgruntled sighs.

Hadi continued, "Now, if I understand your story correctly, you escaped this place once and have been returned. This would lead one to suspect that the fates wish you to be here, would it not?"

"That would lead one to suspect that the darn car had some sort of a homing device," Allie said sarcastically.

"Ah, yes. That is possible," Hadi said. After a pause, he said musingly, "Could it be that your return to this place was created so that we could meet? That, of course, is possible. If so, then it would not offend Allah if we were to leave since we now have met."

Maggie and Allie, still sitting on the floor with their backs against the cold masonry wall, clasped hands. "Maybe that is so, Hadi," Maggie said soothingly. Allie gave her hand an encouraging squeeze. Maggie continued, "How long have you been here? What is this place like? We can't see anything. It appears that there's a door and a tiny window high on the wall. Is that correct?"

"Many questions, dear lady. You are very perceptive with your physical eyes. Now tell me what else you have discovered about this place," Hadi said. "If you will quiet your mind for a moment and just pay attention, much will be learned."

Having little else to do, Maggie closed her eyes and thought for a moment. "I believe this is a masonry structure. I also think that it is quite small, no more than twelve feet by twelve feet. The ceiling appears to be slightly higher than the usual." She was silent for a few more moments, then, "Ugh, I also think there are mice here!"

"Very good!" Hadi said approvingly. "You see, one can learn much without using one's eyes." Then in a regretful voice, "However, I fear there may be rats as well as mice."

Maggie and Allie shivered in unison, "Oooooh!"

"They are not so lovable, yes?" Hadi said. "But, we do not need to be bothered by them. We have only to wish them well and bid them to go elsewhere. They will leave us alone."

"I certainly encourage you to do that," said Allie with a shiver. "In the meantime, could we focus on bidding ourselves to go elsewhere?"

"Ah, yes. You wish to leave this place. If, indeed, it is true that the purpose in your returning here is for us to meet, and we have done that, then there really is no reason for us to remain in this small enclosure. If there is no reason for us to remain here, then it should be quite simple to find ourselves elsewhere." Hadi was speaking low, almost as if to himself.

"It's very difficult to know how to escape from here because we can't see anything," said Maggie in frustration as she began a cautious exploration of the perimeter of the room.

"You haven't told us yet why it is you find yourself imprisoned here." She thought to herself that she even was beginning to sound like Hadi.

"Oh, that. Yes. Here I am. Do you not think that it must be that I have somehow incurred the displeasure of those powerful men?" He responded mysteriously.

"Well, yes. It would appear so," Maggie decided to drop the question because she was beginning to despair of ever receiving a direct answer. After a short silence she said in a small voice, "Hadi, I'm sorry to bring this subject up, but have they given you food. It's been many hours since we've eaten and my insides definitely are complaining."

Allie contributed, "Amen!"

"They bring food in the mornings. Soon it will become light and the sun will come up," Hadi said.

"So, if we are to escape this place before morning probably we need to do so immediately," Allie said. "It'd be easier to get away while it is dark."

"That would seem to be so; however, when we move in harmony with Allah neither light nor darkness are important because we are going with the natural order of things," Hadi said.

Maggie wished she could see this strange man who spouted these pronouncements. She tried to imagine what he might look like. "Well, Hadi, when do you think we'd be in harmony with Allah?"

"Ah, dear lady, that is an excellent question. Sometimes the proper course of action sets itself clearly in front of us; however, sometimes we can only sense and put one foot in front of the other one step at a time, slowly and cautiously. I have not yet received a clear image of the correct course in this situation, either to take action or to remain still. It appears that we need to wait for direction." Hadi said the last slowly and quietly.

As he spoke Maggie noticed that the small opening high on the wall had become a shade lighter. She sighed and leaned back against the cold wall, realizing how very tired she felt. What she wanted more than anything right now was a hot shower, a clean bed and hours of quiet blissful sleep. "It would seem then, Hadi, that we're to remain here a while longer. I do hope that they pay little attention to us today."

"Oh, Mom, you sound exhausted. As a matter of fact, I feel that way too. We've had a long, stressful time with little sleep and food." Allie's voice trailed off, sounding tired and defeated.

"Yes, the light is coming and we need some time. I will sit in silence for a time. You may join me or you may sleep. Our course will be clearer later." So saying, Hadi took a deep breath and was still.

Maggie and Allie propped themselves together against the wall, their bodies and their spirits sagging. Silence descended over the little cell. The only sounds were the deep breathing of the two exhausted women and that of Hadi who was deep in meditation.

Harry Cavanaugh held the receiver away from his face and took a long gulp of the now cold coffee. He sat the cup down as the phone was answered, "Landis here."

"John, this is Harry. Any news?

"No. Nothing new. How about you?" was the discouraged reply.

"Well, nothing good on this end. The McGill women were abducted, held captive somewhere in Hollywood. They escaped. We were on our way to them when they got them again." Harry's voice carried the depth of his disappointment and concern. His voice picked up a little. "We do have an idea of the area they had them in. There's no way of knowing whether or not they returned there, but we're doing a house-to-house inquiry. If we're real lucky we might find them before it's too late."

"Yeah. Too late. Do you have any more information about what these guys are planning. . .other than abducting innocent citizens?" Landis asked.

Harry answered, "Not really. Nothing good, we can be sure of that. It's causing us a great deal of concern that they may be touching in on this college program. Can't be sure whether their interest is only in Andre Fouchet or if there's more to it. Makes a person real uneasy!"

"You got that right.   Uneasy!   Well, keep me posted." Landis signed off.

"Right."   Cavanaugh put the phone down.   In his mind's ear he still could hear Maggie's last words calling to him for help.   "I've got to find her soon," he muttered to himself, "and her daughter, too, of course."

Chapter Eight

Maggie woke with a start. Light was entering through the small high window providing limited illumination. Allie still was slumped against her with her head resting on Maggie's shoulder. Maggie blinked and peered across the room. What she saw did not so much surprise her as command her attention. She always had found it fascinating to match up faces to telephone voices. Now she had the opportunity to match up last night's voice with the rest of the person. Hadi was sitting in the opposite corner of the room with his eyes closed, his back straight and his legs crossed in the traditional meditative posture. His face, in fact, his whole body seemed to be lit by a shimmering light. Maggie closed her eyes again, thinking they were playing tricks on her. For a few moments she felt very peaceful, as if she had no problems at all. It was a lovely feeling, one she had not experienced for a long time. For some reason, she felt rested and refreshed.

"Good morning, dear lady. Did you rest well?" Hadi's voice was soft and comforting.

"Well, yes, I think I did, thank you," Maggie replied. As she spoke Allie stirred, stretched, and opened her eyes.

"Hi, Mom. Hello, Hadi. How are you?" Allie asked sleepily.

"We appear to be in much better condition now," said Maggie. "I wonder how long we slept? How're you feeling, Honey?"

"I feel amazingly well," answered Allie.

"There are times when quantity is not as important as quality," Hadi commented obliquely.

Allie looked at Hadi, ready with a comment about philosophical pontification at this early hour. She saw a small, dark-skinned man, wearing a pale blue turban, still sitting cross-legged in the corner of the room. He appeared to be less than average in height, his wrists, protruding from the sleeves of the loose white shirt he wore, were tanned and bony. His shoulders seemed unusually broad for one so thin. His back was straight and he appeared to be as comfortable as if he were in an easy chair. He returned her look with steady, shining, penetrating deep brown eyes set in a thin bony face. A short goatee-style beard and mustache covered his face. He smiled kindly at her and said, "Truth is true at any hour, dear lady."

Allie's mouth opened and then closed. Her first thought had been that she wished Hadi had turned out to be large and muscular. As a rescuer she had thought that he might be in as much need of help as she and her mother. Now, she sat back in silence wondering if he really had known what was in her mind. She was beginning to think that there might be more to him than met the eye.

Her thoughts were interrupted by a scraping noise and the sound of the lock being turned. As she looked around, the door opened and their ferrety captor entered with a tray of three steaming bowls of food and a large plastic bottle of water. He wore a white bandage on the side of his head and he cast a malevolent look at Maggie and Allie. Wordlessly he sat the tray on the floor and backed hastily out of the room, closing and locking the door.

"Ah, Allah once again has provided us with what we need," Hadi said. He rose and crossed to the tray. Solemnly he handed a bowl to each of them. Then, loudly he said, "*Enchallah!*"

Maggie asked, "What did you say? What does that mean, Hadi?"

Hadi responded, "I was thanking Allah for his constant care and protection, and especially for this food."

The aroma was delicious, but it was unfamiliar to Maggie. "What is this?" she asked as she spooned the hot food into her mouth.

"I think it is couscous and vegetables in a meat broth, probably lamb," said Allie. "Whatever it is, it's simply heavenly. Thank you, Hadi, for offering our thanks too."

As the warm food hit her stomach, Maggie could feel it sending strength and warmth all the way to her toes. They ate in blissful silence for a few moments. As she ate, Maggie looked more closely at their prison. It was much as she had suspected. A masonry structure, concrete block walls, concrete floor, a high ceiling, maybe nine or ten feet high with open wooden rafters. In all it was about twelve feet square. The only door stood near the corner of one wall. The small high window was no more than eighteen inches wide by ten inches high. Except for their bodies and the food tray, the room was completely bare.

"Hadi, probably it was a good idea for us to get some rest before we attempt to leave here; however, now that we've rested, when do you think we can leave?" Allie spoke softly and respectfully to the little man.

"Miss Allie, thank you for that." He continued, "It is not yet time for us to leave. When the time is correct, we will have no difficulty at all in leaving this room. But that time is not yet. To act at the incorrect time will bring only difficulty."

"They're very angry with Allie and me, Hadi," Maggie said. "I fear that they may really harm us if we stay around."

"It is true that they hold anger in their hearts, but they will not harm you yet," he said. "They, too, are waiting." Once again Hadi rose, collected the bowls, replaced them on the tray. He then passed the water bottle first to Maggie.

Maggie drank the cool water gratefully. Making conversation, she asked Hadi, "Tell us about your name. I don't know Arabic. Does your name have a meaning?"

Hadi looked at them with a smile and said, "Ah, dear lady. It is interesting that you ask. I will tell you a story. I am named Hadi. Hadi is a Sufi. It is said that when one is lost in the desert and if one is fortunate, he will meet Hadi. It is necessary that one follow Hadi without question or hesitation. For a long time they may wander through the desert and perhaps the person may spy a shining oasis in a different direction than Hadi is leading him. One then may hesitate and doubt and say to Hadi, 'Hadi, there is an oasis over there.' The person may then leave Hadi and head toward the oasis. The doubt causes Hadi to disappear and the person, upon reaching the area where he saw the oasis, finds it was but a mirage. Soon the person perishes. But perhaps if he had followed Hadi over the next sand dune the real oasis would have been there. The lesson is to follow Hadi in perfect faith and without question. It is good to follow the path of Allah the same way."

Silence followed the story. Each of the three seemed lost in his or her own thoughts. Questions surfaced in Maggie's mind. Who *is* this man? How did he come to be here? Is he to be trusted?

Allie's thoughts were following a similar track. She was torn between trusting him completely and thinking that he was a consummate con artist.

Finally, Maggie said, "A very interesting story, Hadi. You have quite a tradition to live up to." She didn't ask the questions that came to mind.

The peace of the little cell was interrupted by the sound of approaching footsteps, a scraping noise, and then the sound of a key in the lock. They watched as the doorknob turned and the door opened. The Ferret stepped just across the threshold. Motioning to Allie and Maggie, he said, "You two. Come."

Maggie and Allie stood up slowly and awkwardly, their muscles stiff from hours spent on the cold concrete floor. Allie said, "We need to use the bathroom. Please take us there."

The Ferret looked annoyed, but nodded his head. Maggie and Allie glanced at Hadi, who gave them an encouraging smile and then they walked through the door into the sunlit courtyard. Squinting in the brightness, Maggie noticed, across the small enclosure, steps leading down to yet another level. They were joined by the burly man who had taken them from the car last night, Maggie's Bruno. They were led single file by The Ferret and followed by Bruno, up white steps to the level of the garage and then up another level and into the kitchen. No one spoke.

The Ferret led them to a room off the kitchen, probably a maid's room, and indicated a bathroom. Maggie and Allie started to enter the bathroom together, but he caught roughly at Allie's shoulder and held her back while Maggie entered. "Be good, or else," he said and waved an ugly little gun at Allie.

Maggie nodded. In the bathroom she washed her hands and splashed water on her face. She smoothed her unruly hair as best she could and wondered where her purse might be. She looked longingly at the shower but her fear for Allie caused her to hurry out. The Ferret nodded to Allie and waved the gun at Maggie. Allie entered the bathroom, was gone only a few minutes and emerged looking a bit more refreshed.

The Ferret motioned them into the elevator. The elevator ascended and they exited on the level of the living room. The living room had been furnished in the last few hours with a folding table and four folding chairs. Sitting behind the table with his back to the glass wall was Ahmed, the man from the airplane.

He indicated two chairs placed across from him, facing the glass, and said in accented English, "Please, sit down, ladies. I apologize for your accommodations last night. However, your lack of cooperation made it necessary. I hope you were not too uncomfortable."

His voice was cold and flat, negating any courtesy the words might have carried. As she and Allie took their seats, Maggie squinted her eyes against the glare behind him in order to see Ahmed more clearly. He appeared older, or was it more stressed, than she remembered. His face was puffy, with loose skin under his eyes that Maggie had not noticed before. However, the air of menace was more evident than ever.

Maggie gasped as she noticed her own and Allie's purses opened with their contents spilled out on the folding table in front of him. Oh, what she would give for her comb and lipstick right now! There they were, only a few feet away.

Allie asked, "Who are you? Why have you brought us here? What do you want from us?"

Ahmed fastened his cold black eyes on her and said, "You ask too many questions, young woman. You will be silent until I give you permission to speak."

Allie started to reply, but looking at his face, she decided to stay quiet.

Ahmed shifted his gaze to Maggie. His eyes had a flat quality that was disconcerting. It seemed as if his eyes were dead, as if there was nothing at all behind them. Maggie repressed a little shiver and stared back at him. It was difficult to maintain eye contact, but it seemed important not to let him know how frightened she was.

After what seemed a long time, he spoke, "Mrs. McGill, you have given us a great amount of trouble. It has been very annoying. Who are you? Who are you working for? It will do you no good to deny the truth because we will discover what is so. It would be much better for you to be honest with us now."

Maggie looked back at him in bewilderment. Then she sat up straight in her chair and said with dignity, "My name, as you know, is Margaret McGill. I live in Costa Mira, Florida. I am self-employed, a psychotherapist. I'm on vacation, a visit with my daughter. I have no idea what you're talking about and I'm outraged by what's happened since I have been here. I want an explanation from you. More than that, I want an apology and I demand that you release us and return us to our home at once!" Maggie said with more bravado than she felt. She was grateful that her voice held steady and that she was sitting down because she felt quite trembly inside.

Ahmed continued his gaze without blinking. He sighed and said, "So that is how it is. You persist in defying us. That is an unwise choice, madam. We know you have the picture, that is, unless you already have passed it on to your employers. We know you are acquainted with the French couple. We know your daughter is involved with the FLO people. We know you called someone named Harry from the automobile. Who is he? Come now. You cannot expect us to believe that you are only an innocent tourist."

Maggie looked at him in dismay. How could he know about that phone call? Finally, she said, "Harry's an old friend. He knows all about the things that have been happening to us in the past few days. If anything happens to us, you may be sure he'll go to the proper authorities." She hoped this would satisfy Ahmed and perhaps give them some amount of protection.

Ahmed glared at Maggie with an unblinking flat stare, his face expressionless. After a short silence he turned to Allie. "Now, Miss McGill. I want to know your part in this. Have you recruited your mother to work for these people, or did she recruit you? It would be to your advantage to cooperate with us. Just tell us what we want to know, give us the picture and its negative, and we will let you return to your home." He continued staring without blinking and made a small grimace with his mouth that was intended to be a smile.

Allie gave him a disdainful look and said, "Surely you can not believe that my mother and I have anything or know anything that could be of value to you. She told you the truth. My mother is here for a visit. She and I have no idea what you're talking about. I repeat her request, that you release us and permit us to return to our home, and, by the way, that you return our property to us." Allie indicated the purses and their contents. "Or do you and your men wish to wear our lipstick?" she said with a sneer.

Ahmed snorted. He glared at her angrily and banged his closed fist on the folding table that jumped, rattling the objects on it. "You. . .you!" He collected himself with effort and then said coldly, "You will regret your decisions to defy us." Then to the Ferret and the other man, "Take them back and lock them in." As they were rising from their chairs, he swept the contents of the purses into one and shoved both purses into Maggie's arms. "Take these. We have no use for them." He turned his back to them and stared out the window.

Maggie clutched the purses gratefully as she left the room, walking behind Allie, with Bruno following her. Down in the elevator, through the kitchen, down the steps. Ferret unlocked the door and pushed the two of them into their prison. This time, Maggie and Allie stumbled but were able to remain upright. They stood awkwardly for a moment allowing their eyes to adjust to the dim light.

Hadi was sitting cross-legged in the corner, as if he had not moved since they left. "Ah, dear ladies, it is, indeed, good to see you once again. Please to sit and make yourselves comfortable. Then, if you wish, tell me of the events of your absence."

They slumped down in unison, grateful to be enveloped in his peaceful presence. They looked first at Hadi, then at each other and back to Hadi. Maggie began, "Oh, Hadi. It's awful. That nasty man, I think his name is Ahmed, that nasty man thinks we're working for his enemies. He thinks we have a picture that we don't have and that we know something we don't. He wouldn't believe anything we told him. He was furious. I'm afraid of what he might do." For the first time, tears sprang from her eyes. She wiped them away quickly with the back of her hand.

Allie continued, "Hadi, it doesn't look good for us. That is an *evil* man and he's very angry with us. I'm afraid I made him even madder, but he annoyed me so. Oh, Hadi, we must find a way out of here!"

Hadi looked at each of them and said, "It was a distressing interview, was it not? It would seem that it would be good to leave here. We will do so at the proper time."

Maggie and Allie looked at one another with a sigh. Then Maggie realized she still was clutching the two purses. "Well, at least we got these back. That was the one good thing about the interview." She dumped the purses and their contents on the floor as she and Allie sat down and began to sort them. Combs, lipsticks, keys, a couple of emery boards, a few chocolate bars, their wrappers frayed, wallets—money and credit cards untouched.

Suddenly, Maggie asked, "Where's my camera? I usually carry it in my purse. Did they take it? Could they be looking for one of my pictures?"

Allie shrugged, "Who knows? Did you have the camera with you in the condo? Remember. You dropped the film at the drug store. Maybe you put the camera in the glove box. But, wait, where is my cell phone? Didn't I have it with me?"

Maggie went back in her mind to that morning at the shopping mall. Could it only have been yesterday? She was retracing their actions. She said, "You're right. I must have put the camera, the fresh film and the receipt for the processing in the glove box. I was intending to reload the camera when we were out of the sunshine. But I forgot about it. About your phone, you used it to call Ed, remember? I think we left it in the car, too."

"Well, that's good. At least, they haven't taken anything." After a silence Allie added ruefully, "Except, that is, our freedom!"

"Yes, and our peace of mind," Maggie said.

"Peace of mind," Hadi interjected, "Now that is an interesting phrase. How can that be taken from you? It is inside you and you have the choice—to permit it to leave or to hold to it. When our faith is strong, then nothing can take peace from us."

Allie sighed and said, "Hadi, I'm sure that's okay for a saint or something, but we're human. We have feelings and right now we're scared. I don't like even to say this, but I'm afraid they mean to do away with us when they get what they're after or if they decide we can't give it to them. I don't think they intend let us go whatever happens. It's scary and it's not easy to be peaceful right now."

Hadi replied, "What you say may be so, dear lady. I have some knowledge of these people and I agree that they do not wish any of us well. However, what they wish and what Allah wills may not be in congruence. That is, they may wish us evil, but Allah may wish us good. We must remember where the real power lies."

Suddenly the door was thrown open and two bodies landed in a heap on the floor between them. Maggie and Allie gasped. The bodies began to move and groan. The three prisoners hurried forward to help their visitors to upright positions. As the newcomers sat up, Maggie exclaimed, "Andre! Brigitte! How did you get here? Are you all right?"

Allie asked, "What happened to you? Everyone's been worried."

Andre and Brigitte Fouchet blinked, their eyes adjusting to the dimmer light in the little room. They looked blankly at Maggie, Allie and Hadi. With a shake of his head, Andre looked at Maggie and said, "You? You were on the airplane? Yes, I remember now. You were on the airplane." His English was much better than Maggie remembered. He shifted his gaze to Allie, a puzzled look on his face. "You look familiar, but I do not know. . .."

Allie interrupted, "The FLO party. We didn't meet, but you may have seen us there. I am Allie McGill and this is my mother, Maggie."

"You were there? You both were there?" His puzzled look cleared as he remembered. He looked again at Maggie and said, "You at the party. I saw you for a moment. Then you were gone. I had forgotten. Well, you seem to know our names. How do you do." First Andre and then Brigitte reached across and shook hands with Maggie and Allie.

With his arm around Brigitte, Andre turned to Hadi. "And you? I think we have not met. My name is Andre Fouchet and this is my wife, Brigitte."

Hadi inclined his head, smiled and introduced himself, "Mohammed Hadi El Kabir. You may call me Hadi."

As he shook Hadi's hand, Andre looked at him strangely and intently. Then he said, "How do you do, Hadi. You have an interesting name."

"That is so, sir. Why do you say so?" Hadi asked in flawless French that Allie followed only with difficulty and Maggie could follow not at all. Allie translated softly.

Hearing her native language being spoken, Brigitte raised her head and listened, some of the fatigue leaving her face.

Andre looked inquiringly into Hadi's eyes and said, "Hadi is the name given to the Sufi trickster God. Are you a Sufi?"

"Yes, I follow the teachings of the Sufi tradition. So you know about my culture," Hadi said again in fluent French. "That, indeed, is interesting."

"Yes, it's been my life's work to study the cultures of the Middle East," replied Andre. Maggie and Allie were grateful that Andre now spoke in English. Harry was right. Andre's English was very good.

"It is indeed fortunate that we have met." Turning to Maggie and Allie, Hadi said, in English this time, "It may be that we have been waiting for these, our friends, to join us. If so, and if it is the will of Allah, then we may perhaps leave this place." He grinned and added, "The floor? It is becoming somewhat hard, no?" Then he turned to Brigitte and greeted her in French, inclining his head toward her to show his concern.

Brigitte replied in French, at first mumbling slowly, but then seeming to gain strength and encouragement from his concern, she spoke more clearly and rapidly. It was apparent that she was exhausted and terrified by her ordeal. Maggie reached over, took her hand, and gave it an encouraging squeeze. Brigitte turned to her, *"Merci, merci."* Any English she may have known seemed to have disappeared during her imprisonment.

The five prisoners talked in low tones, becoming acquainted and sharing the details of their recent adventures in an increasingly workable mixture of French and English. Brigitte and Andre told of Brigitte's daylight abduction from a San Francisco street corner, of the ransom telephone call to Andre, of Andre's attempt to rescue her, a sort of treasure hunt from phone booth to phone booth, and his subsequent abduction from a dock area in San Francisco.

Talked out, silence reigned. Suddenly, Maggie asked, "How did they know about Harry?" Then she stopped and put her hand over her mouth and looked at Allie. In their account of the last few days, Maggie and Allie had omitted any reference to Harry Cavanaugh and the CIA.

Andre sat up and asked, "Who is Harry?"

Allie gave her mother a smile and said, "I really think it's okay to tell them about Harry. I don't think it matters one way or the other." So they told about Harry.

Andre released a sigh and said, "I, too, have held something back. I, too, think it really does not matter now whether you know about it or not. After Brigitte had been taken, I was beside myself. I had just received a phone call in my hotel room making demands of me, when a man appeared at the door. His name was John Landis and he said he worked for the CIA, that they had tried to protect Brigitte and me. Together we came to some conclusions about who it may have been who had kidnapped Brigitte, what they wanted and we developed a plan to rescue her." He paused and looked lovingly at his wife. Then he continued ruefully, "As you see, it didn't work exactly as we'd planned. The plan was quite simple. I was to wear a tracking device and follow the instructions from the kidnappers until I had been led to Brigitte. At which time, Landis and his group would come to the rescue." Andre paused again and shook his head. "They were very angry when they discovered the bug. I think they wanted to kill both of us then and there, but so far they haven't done so. Early this morning they put us into the back of a car and brought us here. Where are we, by the way?

"Oh, we are at a house in the Hollywood hills," Allie said.

Again silence fell upon the little group. All except Hadi slumped against the walls. Brigitte rested her head on Andre's shoulder and sighed. Maggie and Allie propped themselves against one another. Hadi remained in his corner, his back straight, his legs crossed, his eyes closed, his breathing slow, deep and even.

Chapter Nine

The inner tube bounced as it floated down the river. Maggie was suspended in it, her behind hanging down in the cold water. As she watched, small floes of ice drifted by. She was freezing. Most of all, her derriere was cold, in fact, it was freezing. Parts of her were becoming numb. She shivered.

Maggie woke shivering. She opened her eyes to find herself still in the little room with her fellow prisoners. She *was* cold. The room was chilly. Most of all, the concrete was frigid and her behind had gone numb from sitting in one position on the hard floor. She shifted uncomfortably. The movement roused Allie who groaned a little and sat up also. In the semi-darkness the small oblong window above their heads was now only a little lighter than the dark walls. Across the room she could just see the Fouchets still asleep and in the opposite corner, Hadi sat, unmoving.

In his soft singsong voice Hadi asked, "Ah, dear ladies, you have come back. Welcome. Did you rest well?"

Maggie and Allie stretched and flexed cramped muscles. "Well, yes, Hadi, I think we did," answered Allie. "And you? Did you rest?"

"Hadi rests in the arms of Allah, always," was the reply.

At the sound of voices Andre gave a little start and sat up. Brigitte also awoke and stretched. "What time is it? Is it late?" he asked.

Through the gloom Hadi smiled at Maggie and Allie, looked at Andre and Brigitte and said, "It is time, I think, for us to find a new place to be. Shall we be out of this place now?"

"Oh, my, yes! Let's," breathed Maggie.

Allie nodded her head vehemently.

Gently, in French to Brigitte, Hadi said, "And you, dear one, are you now able to leave here?"

Softly she answered, *"Oui, oui."*

Allie said, "But, Hadi, how? How can we get out of here? There's no way out. There's only the door and it is locked."

"That is true, dear lady. That is true. At the same time we know now it is the will of Allah that we leave. We had only to wait for all of us to be here, for a little rest and for darkness. Now that all three events have occurred, there no longer is a reason for us to be here. Allah will guide our steps," Hadi said matter of matter-of-factly. "Let us delay no more."

The five prisoners stood up, stretching and testing cold and cramped muscles. "It would seem to me that a very small person might be able to propel herself through that small opening on the wall. Once she arrives on the outside of this room, if she looks diligently, she might then find a key near the door that would open the door and then we all will be able to walk out." Once again Hadi spoke with complete confidence.

Maggie could feel four sets of eyes turned in her direction. "Are you saying that I could crawl through that little window?"

she asked tremulously. "If that's your idea, I'm afraid we're sunk. I've spent many hours contemplating that window and its possibilities. I do not have wings and I certainly can't reach that high. Even if I could get up there, I doubt that I could open it, and even if I could do that, how would I get down on the outside?"

Hadi replied, "Please, please, calm yourself, dear lady. If M. Fouchet will allow me, I will stand on his shoulders and thus open the window. If necessary, I will break the glass. However, I fear I would not fit through the opening."

Maggie looked at Hadi. Even though he was a small man, his shoulders were broad. Looking at the window, she could see that he was correct. She considered her own form. A bit round in places, but basically petite. She might be able to squeeze herself through it.

Hadi went on, "The four of us will lift you high enough to go through the window. This room is built against the hillside. Have you not noticed the difference in the temperatures of the different walls? The drop on the outside should be quite short; however, I will, just for you, sacrifice my turban. If I unwind it, you may use it to support your descent to the ground."

Maggie took a deep breath. "Yes, yes, I see. It just might work. Okay. Let's go for it."

Andre and Hadi stood under the window. Andre bent over with his head resting against the wall. Hadi then climbed on his shoulders and slowly Andre stood upright. The three women stood around them, steadying them. Hadi now was nearly chest high to the window. He worked silently for a few moments, and then with an "Ooof!" and a scraping sound, the window opened out, hinged at the top edge. "Quickly now. Let me down."

On the floor Hadi said softly to Maggie, "I was correct. The ground is no more than four or five feet below the window. Do you want the turban for security?"

"No, no. I think I can jump that far. I wouldn't want to desecrate your turban unnecessarily," she said with a little forced laugh.

"Very good. Now. We shall built a pyramid, no? Andre and I on the bottom. Brigitte and Allie above us." As Hadi talked the others followed his directions. "Now, dear lady, if you would just climb up us, as if we were a stair. There. Good. Good."

Maggie found herself standing on the bent shoulders of Brigitte and Allie. Before her, the open window seemed pitifully small. It was, however, just at her waist. The only way she could move through it was headfirst. Cautiously, she turned with her back to the window and edged her head and shoulders through the opening. With a little grunt she hoisted her body up so that she was sitting on the sill with her feet and legs still inside and her upper body leaning out, hanging onto the edge of the window itself. She looked down. In the dim light it appeared that the ground was not so very far away. Slowly she scooted her bottom out, still clinging to the window with her hands. When her feet were on the windowsill, she began to walk them down the side of the wall, hanging on to the window for dear life. Before she knew it, first one foot and then another touched solid ground. She was out! And without mishap!

The air smelled wonderful. There were stars over her head. Hallelujah! Now to release the others. Carefully, as quietly as she could, Maggie inched down the hill all the time touching the wall of the little building. She rounded a corner and along the wall of the building. Near the next corner was the door. She stood quietly for a moment, listening. Nothing. No sounds from the big house.   She approached the door and looked around. Now to find the key, if Hadi was right about its being here.   A half-moon high in the eastern sky gave limited illumination.   She passed her hands around the edge of the doorframe, standing on tiptoe, reaching as high as she could. Nothing. On her knees, again using Braille. To the left of the door. Nothing. To the right. Only a planting pocket filled with rocks. A large stone. There, under the stone, a key. Maggie's hands were shaking. She stopped and took some deep breaths. Now quietly, quietly, to fit the key in the lock. At last the door opened. The others welcomed her with hugs and pats on the shoulder.

"Allie, where are our purses?" Maggie whispered. Allie handed Maggie her purse.   Maggie draped it around her shoulder and neck so that it would be out of the way as much as possible.

Silently, they filed out of the little room.   Softly Hadi closed the door behind them. Just then they heard voices above their heads. Someone was talking softly on one of the upper terraces. Hadi touched each one quickly and led them back, up the hill behind their prison, away from the house. They found themselves on a sharp ridge of ground. Below them to the left spread the Los Angeles basin, its lights glittering like regimented stars. Below them on the other side was the street. The drop to the left probably was not negotiable even in daylight. Certainly it was not so after dark. The street to their right seemed much too exposed. Hadi led them slowly along the sharp ridge for about three hundred yards where the land broadened into open country.   In the weak moonlight they marched single file upward, away from the houses.

Maggie was grateful that Hadi had chosen to lead them away from the house and the obvious choice of the street and the other houses. Their recent abortive escape still was all too vivid in her memory. She could not see very much, but what she did see was daunting. Rough, open country covered with prickly scrub growth and above their heads on the side of the mountain was the huge HOLLYWOOD sign, its letters glowing dimly in the moonlight. Where were they going? What was on the other side of this mountain?

Maggie found herself out of breath frequently as they climbed. They stopped to rest from time to time. It was understood, although no one mentioned it, that Brigitte was the most fragile of them and the rests were for her benefit. However, Maggie was extremely grateful for each breather. She promised herself a regular exercise program when she returned home. She could hardly remember her home and her office. That part of her life had taken on a strange dream-like quality, like a movie watched long ago and dimly remembered.

Hadi moved ahead steadily, without haste, seemingly effortlessly. Yet, they were covering ground quickly. When she looked back, Maggie was surprised to note that the Los Angeles basin with its lights had disappeared. There was only a glow on the horizon behind and the nine huge letters above to remind them that they still were in the city.

They stopped for another rest. Maggie sat on a rock, breathing heavily. Allie gasped between breaths, "Are you doing okay, Mom? This is a pretty arduous hike."

"Yes." Breath. "Yes, I'm okay." Breath. "Just a little out of shape," Maggie answered.

"Ah, dear ladies, it is a glorious night for a walk, is it not?" Hadi said softly in his singsong voice. He motioned above their heads. Overhead the stars blazed brightly in the black velvet night. The moon silvered all objects it touched. Then Maggie noticed a cool breeze on her face. He was right. It was a beautiful night. However, calling this scramble a walk was stretching positive thinking to the limit!

They moved on, continuing to climb upward. "Hadi," Allie gasped, "Where're we going? Do you know?"

Hadi answered, "We are going where Allah leads. We do not need to know more."

"But," Allie started to reply, but saved her breath.

Brigitte's steps were becoming noticeably more faltering. She leaned heavily on Andre, their progress became slower and slower. While Maggie and Allie had the advantage of being dressed in jeans, sweaters and walking shoes, Brigitte wore the short skirt, blazer and light flat shoes she was wearing when she left her hotel for a short shopping trip.

"Madame Fouchet," Hadi said at their next rest, "I know this is a difficult trek for you. But you must know that we need to put as much space between our captors and ourselves as quickly as possible. For all of us, it is important that we continue. If you will let the earth help you it will be easier. As you place each foot, feel the earth give it back to you. Feel the earth pushing you on."

"Oui, oui," murmured Brigitte. "We go." Brigitte seemed to strengthen with Hadi's words. She drew a long breath, stood up and started walking upward. Andre hurried to her side and took her arm, but she shook it off and walked resolutely ahead.

Maggie did not know how far they had climbed. She had ceased looking around, but focused her attention only on putting one foot in front of the other. Just when she thought she could go no farther, it seemed that she got a second wind, it seemed that the earth was helping, was supporting her. Amazing!

At the next rest, Maggie looked back. The glittering Los Angeles basin had returned. They were high on the hill under the HOLLYWOOD sign now. From this vantage it was impossible to discern which of the houses was their former prison. The houses were only tiny dark spaces between the lights. Somewhere a dog was barking. Otherwise the world seemed strangely silent.

"We're on Mt. Lee," Allie said in an awed voice. "We're heading for the bloody sign! There's a road up there. If we can just make it to the top. I know there's a road." She rose and started walking again. The others followed one by one, Brigitte and Andre bringing up the rear. A call from behind. They turned to see Andre holding Brigitte in his arms.

"She is feeling very weak," he said. "It has been a long time since she has eaten."

The others rushed back and surrounded the couple. They sat her on the ground. Allie and Maggie chafed her hands, encouraging her, hoping to strengthen her. Hadi arrived and produced the plastic water bottle. It still was nearly full. "Oh, Hadi, how bright of you," said Allie. He poured a few drops into the bottle cap and put it to Brigitte's lips.

"Slowly, slowly," he said.

It was then that Maggie remembered the chocolate bars in her purse. "Here," she said, offering one to Hadi.

"Thank you, dear lady. We will wait a few moments and then we will offer madam a small piece. In the desert it is important to drink and eat very slowly." They continued nursing Brigitte, giving her small amounts of water and finally a small square of the chocolate. At last she lifted her head and began to brighten. Slowly they gave her the rest of the chocolate bar.

"Merci," she said. *"Merci."* Brigitte attempted to rise.

Hadi put out a hand to restrain her. "Please, madam. Please sit for a while. Let us consider the situation and our next step."

It was then that the others noticed the lightening of the eastern sky. Soon it would be light. That would make their traveling much easier. But it also would expose them to every eye.

"Brigitte is exhausted. There are others of us who also could use a rest. Perhaps we should find a safe spot and send someone for help," Allie suggested.

Hadi smiled at her and agreed, "That is an excellent suggestion."

Together Hadi and Allie left, looking for a resting place. The other three sat on the ground, grateful for the time out. Maggie lay back on the dry earth and looked up at the sky that was changing from gray to pink-streaked blue. For the first time she noticed the coolness of the air. Her thoughts wandered dreamily and her eyes became heavy. A rustling sound jerked her awake. Hadi and Allie were returning.

"We've found a spot, not too far from here. It will give us protection from the sun and seclusion, also," Allie said. They stood up, Andre supporting Brigitte. They proceeded around the hill, climbing only slightly. The rising sun cast long shadows ahead of them. After about a twenty-minute hike they came to a slight declivity in the side of the hill. The depression apparently had caught more moisture than the hillside and the scrub oaks were larger and denser. Hadi leading the way, they crawled through the heavy growth into a small space enclosed on all sides by vegetation.

"This is perfect," Maggie said looking around. "One would have to know it is here to find it."

"Exactly," said Allie. They sat down gratefully. The floor of their refuge was covered with fallen leaves. After some discussion, it was decided that Hadi and Allie should go for help. They were in better condition physically. They divided two of Maggie's chocolate bars five ways. Then Allie stood up and said, "Now, you all get some rest. We will be back soon with good news."

"Honey, I love you. I...," Maggie's voice trailed off.

"Yeah, Mom, I know. I'll be back very soon. I love you, too."

Hadi crawled out through the leaves with Allie close behind. Once out of the copse, Allie and Hadi turned resolutely up hill toward the huge sign. They soon found that the sign was farther away than Allie had thought. They trudged doggedly on.

There was silence in the little copse for a while. Brigitte lay back on the soft leaves and closed her eyes. Andre sat quietly for a while, and then he said to Maggie, "We may as well get some rest. We don't know what will happen next." He lay back beside Brigitte and sighed. On the other side of the enclosure Maggie also lay down and closed her eyes. It was good to be horizontal again. It had been an arduous night. She didn't like to admit how weary she was.

The Ferret shifted from one foot to the other while the cook filled five bowls with hot food. He wondered why they bothered to feed these infidels if they were to die anyway. The tray was heavy already and he motioned for Bruno to bring the water jug. Together they walked out of the kitchen, down the stairs, into the sunny courtyard in front of the garden shed. The Ferret sat the tray on the balustrade while he hunted for the key. It was not there! Muttering he expanded his search. Still no key. Taking out his gun, he tested the door to the shed. It opened without a sound. Cautiously he stepped inside. They were gone! Muttering curses, he ran up the steps into the kitchen and grabbed the telephone. Then he stopped. Ahmed would be furious. This would be the second time those women had escaped them.   The cook's look contained a question. Bruno stared at him without a word. He had no choice. They would talk if he didn't. Drawing a deep breath, he punched in the numbers.

"Ahmed? They are gone."

Sounds of vituperation came through the phone and filled the kitchen. The cook turned his back and busied himself with the washing up.

"No. No. I don't know. The door was unlocked. They just aren't there." He listened a while longer. Then he replaced the telephone. He turned to Bruno, "Come on. We must search for them. We must find out what happened, how they escaped."

Together he and Bruno checked the inside of the little room. They discovered the open window. The Ferret shook his head, wondering how they had managed.   Then they checked the garage. Nothing. The cars stood silent. The Ferret replaced his gun and they walked out and down the street.   Nothing. Finally, they returned to the garden shed and walked around its perimeter, scrambling up and down the uneven ground.   They discovered footprints leading up the spine of the ridge. Cursing to himself, The Ferret returned to the kitchen and reported what he had discovered.

"They won't have gone far," Ahmed said. "Those women will slow them down. Go after them. Bring them back. We will deal with them!" The Ferret listened for a while longer, then, motioning to Bruno to follow, he ran down the steps, into the courtyard, around the shed and started up the ridge toward open country.

Chapter Ten

Allie stopped to catch her breath. Her mouth was cottony dry. She thought longingly of the water jug they had left in the copse. She swayed, her knees feeling shaky. "Ah, dear lady. You are tired, no?" Hadi asked.

"I am tired, yes," said Allie. "And thirsty, and hungry. Hadi, I had no idea this mountain was so big!" She looked at Hadi. He was standing a few feet above her, his feet planted firmly on the hillside, his breathing smooth and even. Didn't he ever get tired?

"Wait, Shhh! I think I hear . . . Yes I do. I heard a car up there!" Allie's spirits picked up. She started the scramble toward the sound she had heard.

"Slowly. Slowly, please. We must proceed carefully," Hadi warned.

Allie checked her pace and climbed more slowly, but steadily. Ahead of them was what appeared to be a wall of huge boulders, some of them garage size or larger. The two picked their way around and over these rocks, scrambling, holding on

119

to one another. At last they found their way through a saddle formed by two huge boulders and just above them they saw a road guardrail. Allie was about to scramble up when she felt Hadi's hand on her shoulder. She turned. He put his finger to his lips.

She looked up. What she saw made her heart sink. A long black automobile was moving slowly along the road. Its windows were down and through the passenger side window she could see a turbaned head. "Damnation!" she muttered. Allie and Hadi sat in the heavy shadows, peeking through the rocks for a while. Every few minutes another black car would pass, its occupants peering out over the landscape, sometimes with binoculars.

While they watched, two bicyclists stopped, wheeled their bikes off the road and parked them behind a boulder only feet from where Allie and Hadi lay. Then the cyclists walked across the road to admire the view. Before she could say anything, Hadi had scrambled down to the bikes, rifled their knapsacks and returned with a treasure of fruit, trail mix, a small thermos and two large canteens of water. He opened a small nylon bag to disclose sandwiches, six beautiful, thick sandwiches! A bonanza!

Silently, Hadi motioned their retreat. Quickly they scrambled down, away from the dangerous road. They sat down in comparative safety behind another huge boulder. They divided the food between them, stuffing fruit into pockets, strapping the canteens and the nylon bag to their bodies. Wordlessly, they moved fast, crouching low, running, sliding down the mountain they had worked so hard to climb.

Harry Cavanaugh picked up the telephone. "Yes."

"Harry? Joe. We've found a house that might be it. Up near Griffith Park. Big. White. Looks like it's still under construction. Neighbors say there've been lights at night. Cars coming and going. What do you want us to do?"

Harry thought for a moment, "Sounds like it could be it. Good work. Can you get around it? Surround it?"

"Don't know how, Harry. It's perched on the edge and it's straight down from there. I'd have to have wings to get on that side. It's surrounded on the street side by walls. No way really to get close without knocking on the door."

"Okay, then. Let's do it. You say it looks like it's under construction? Get someone up there in a utility truck or something. Building inspector. That's it. Send a building inspector in to take a look," Harry said. "Let's see what we can find."

"Gotcha, Harry.

Harry replaced the receiver and sighed. Waiting and not knowing was hell. What would they find in the house, if it was the house? Once again, he remembered the airplane, the tousled blonde head; he remembered the light in her eyes and the warmth of her smile as she thanked him. He remembered Maggie and Allie tugging the luggage off the conveyor. He remembered them on the loggia at the beach club. Initially fierce and suspicious. Then bright, quick, intelligent. He remembered how a shaft of sunlight had touched the top of her head, creating a golden halo around it. Harry sighed. This case was getting to him!

Maggie stirred and sat up, and glanced at her watch. It was after two. She had slept for hours. Then she remembered Allie and Hadi. Where could they be? Concern and panic begin to build. This won't do! Maggie took deep breaths and told herself that those two would be protected and soon would arrive back with good news.

Brigitte was sleeping peacefully, but Andre stretched and opened his eyes. "Hello," he said quietly. "You are awake?"

Maggie nodded and smiled. She and Andre talked, speaking softly, speculating on what might be happening outside of their haven. "Andre, do you have any idea why these people have done this to us? You're the expert on Middle Eastern affairs. Do you know who they are? What they want?" Maggie asked.

Andre was thoughtful. "I have been puzzling about that. I was approached by the Foreign Study people to be on their staff. Brigitte and I haven't been married very long. She'd never been outside of France. I thought it'd be a restful trip for us, an adventure, a sort of honeymoon."

Andre continued, "Some honeymoon! Poor Brigitte. I've been very worried about her. Her exhaustion is as much emotional as it is physical. She's been very frightened." He looked tenderly at her, then continued, "Apparently it's a terrorist organization. The ultimate goal of terrorism, of course, is to create so much chaos and violence that the government cannot protect its citizens. Then the populace loses faith in their government and there's anarchy. Out of the turmoil the people will embrace any form of government that can restore order. The terrorists believe that then their side will prevail. It's a dreadful thing, terrorism. Its targets are the innocents who are unable to protect themselves. It's a cowardly sort of warfare."

Maggie was thoughtful, "If these people are terrorists, why target us? We're only individuals. I'd think they'd do something spectacular, like blowing up a bridge or something."

"Exactly," Andre replied. "I assume that we're seen as a threat to some plot they've concocted. I don't for a moment think that we're the primary targets. I believe that we've gotten in their way in some manner we don't know."

Maggie mused, "What could that possibly be?"

"Did you say they were asking you about a picture? What sort of picture do you think they meant? A photo? A painting?" Andre asked.

"Oh, I think they meant a photo. Ahmed mentioned a negative so it must be a photo. But I can't image what photo," Maggie answered.

"Did you say your daughter is a photographer? Could it be something she has that she doesn't realize she has?"

"Well, you know, they did break into her house and search everywhere. Apparently they didn't find what they were looking for. Of course, her professional negatives are stored at the lab. But they didn't ask *her* about the picture. They asked *me!* As if they thought I knew what they were talking about," Maggie explained.

"You say that nothing out of the ordinary happened until you reached California?" Andre asked.

"No. Nothing. Nothing at all. Of course, Ahmed was on the flight from Florida. I thought I noticed a lot of turbans around, but nothing *happened* until after we arrived in San Francisco," Maggie said thoughtfully.

Andre said, "Could you innocently have snapped a photo on this trip that might have something in it that you don't know is in it, but which is threatening to them?"

"Well, yes, I suppose I could have. I do take a lot of snapshots," Maggie answered. "But, I've no idea what it may have been. Mostly I take pictures of Allie and of scenery," she added. "But, what about you, Andre? Why should you present a threat to them?" Maggie asked.

"I am not sure, of course. But, I think that's a little less of a mystery than your case. I do know a lot about terrorism, you know. Apparently, my presence here in this country is somehow a threat to them. What it is that I might know, or what I might discover by being here that frightens them I have no idea." Andre shook his head in puzzlement. "It's clear that they wish me to leave the country."

Maggie nodded sympathetically. They sat quietly for a few moments, and then Maggie spoke again, "Andre, when you met Hadi you responded as if you knew something about him. Had you met him or heard about him before?"

Andre smiled, "Hadi is very interesting, isn't he? I haven't quite figured him out. But to answer your question, no, I had not met him before yesterday. But heard about him . . . now that's something else. I really don't know how to answer that. You see, Hadi is the name of the trickster, the Sufi equivalent to the Native American 'Coyote' or the Norse God, Loki, or the Native American *heyeohkah*. Many spiritual traditions have a trickster God whose job it is to trick or jolt a person out of their ordinary reality into an awareness of the presence of God. Now, our Hadi seems . . ."

Andre broke off as a rustling in the foliage caused them to quiet their conversation. The rustling became louder and Allie's head appeared, followed by the rest of her and then Hadi. Maggie breathed a huge sigh of relief and a tear sprang to her eye. Allie looked whole, real and vibrant to Maggie. "Oh, you're back. I'm *so* glad to see you," she said, her voice tremulous with relief and gratitude. Whatever else might happen Maggie felt very happy. Thank you.

Allie put her arms around her mother in a big hug. "Hi, Mom. Back from the wars!" she said with a little laugh. "We have good news and bad news!"

Andre and Maggie looked at them questioningly. At the sound of voices, Brigitte stretched, opened her eyes and sat up.

"Tell us the bad news first," Maggie said soberly.

Hadi spoke, "The bad news, dear lady, is that Ahmed's people are patrolling the road. We cannot get close to the road without being seen. We were not able to find help."

"Dear me!" Maggie said. "What is the good news?"

In response, the two scouts unloaded their treasure-trove of food. "I am afraid that there are two bicyclists who will have a hungry ride down the mountain. However, I think their souls will forgive us. I asked Allah to give them a special blessing," Hadi said.

As he spoke Hadi divided the food. He gave each person half a sandwich and a handful of grapes. He said, "We will conserve our food. Even though we have been exerting much, it is good to eat small amounts. When each finishes his food, we will each have three swallows of water. Allah has been good to grant us a bountiful supply. *Enchallah!*"

Allie and Maggie echoed, "*Enchallah!*" They ate in respectful silence and then solemnly passed the water bottle around.

"Except for Allie coming through those bushes this is the best thing I have seen in a long while," Maggie said. "But what are we to do? We can't go back. Now we can't go forward. Any ideas?"

"Well, yes. We do have a plan of sorts," Allie said. "You're correct. We can't go back. If Ahmed's people are on that road, they must've discovered that we came this way. I'd be surprised if they weren't searching the mountain for us on foot. That road's not a safe place for us either. It'd be foolhardy for us to follow it for help. However, if we could cross it tonight and walk to the north all night we should come to some sort of civilization soon. They wouldn't imagine that we'd be so foolish as to keep going on foot. That, I think, is our ace in the hole. This is a well-hidden spot right here. We have some supplies. If any of us does not want to risk the overland trek, then they might be quite safe here with some food and water. Hopefully those of us who go can get help and come back soon."

They were quiet for a moment. No one liked the idea of them separating; however, all were thinking about Brigitte. Could she make such a difficult hike?

Maggie thought about herself. She knew the trip would be exhausting. Even though she was feeling better right now, she remembered her exhaustion of this morning. She wondered if she could make another demanding hike so soon. She decided that she'd rather take her chances on the trail than remain here, where she would feel trapped. Playing a passive role never had appealed to Maggie. Besides, not knowing what was happening would be too difficult to handle.

She had just reached this decision when Brigitte spoke using French when her English failed her, "Please, please. I wish to go. Now that I have rested, now that I am free and with friends, now that I have food, I know I can make the hike. Please, Andre, please, we go."

Andre looked at the other three and said, "If Brigitte wants to give it a try, I agree. I don't want to stay here. We will go. However, we'll go only on the condition that should we not be able to continue, you'll go ahead at that point without us. Wherever we might be at that time, we'd wait there for rescue."

Hadi gazed at Andre and Brigitte for a few moments. Then he said, "We will rest until dark." He sat back against a small tree trunk, crossed his legs and closed his eyes.

The others looked at each other, then without comment, each one leaned back, closed his or her eyes and rested.

Maggie worried behind her closed eyes. Could she make the hike? How about Brigitte? Even though rest and food had helped she still looked frail and weak.

Chapter Eleven

"Cavanaugh here," Harry said into the telephone.

"Harry. This is Joe. I checked out the house. I think it must be the one."

"You *think* it must be? What d'you mean? What'd you find?" Harry asked in exasperation.

"The guys went in, you know, like you said, as inspectors. The only person there said he was the cook. Didn't speak much English. Our guys went all over the place. There was hardly any furniture. A bedroom that you should see. Folding table and chairs in the living room. That was about all, except, get this—a bright red Ferrari in the garage!" Joe said the last with glee.

"Really! Interesting. Nothing else?" Harry asked.

"Well, down from the kitchen there was a sort of garden storage shed. The door was standing open. There was a tiny window high on the wall. It was open, too. The shed was clean except for a couple of things. One of those little plastic sticks, you know, like you stir coffee with.   It had Trans-Global Airlines written on it.

"Bingo!" said Harry excitedly.   "That's the airline the McGill woman came to L.A. on."

"Wait.   There's more.   There was a matchbook from Brandon's.   You know.   That restaurant in Malibu.   One more thing.   The shed had a little courtyard.   In the courtyard was a tray of food—*five* bowls of some sort of soup.   Just sitting there. Funny, huh?" Joe said.

"Funny?   Best break we've had in a while.   Good work, Joe.   Anything more?"

"Well, Harry.   We took a look around that shed.   There'd been some traffic around it.   It looks like a few folks walked out the back way, up the ridge.   What do you think about that?"

"Remind me to give you a raise.   That's just great.   Now the question is.   Where'd they go?   Did they go on their own or were they escorted?"   Harry thought he didn't want to think what their being escorted out the back way might mean.   "Joe, could we get some people up on that ridge.   See if we can track these folks down."

"Sure, Harry.   We'll keep in touch."

"Thanks, Joe."

The Ferret's steps were becoming slower and slower as his breathing became more labored.   He and Bruno were climbing the mountain toward the large HOLLYWOOD sign.   The sun was hot and they had nothing to drink.   The Ferret stopped and sat on a rock, motioning Bruno to do the same.   The first several hundred yards of their hike had been easy.   There were obvious tracks in the dirt.   He had started energetically, confident that they would find their escapees quickly and easily.   Now, he was feeling discouraged.   Only his fear of Ahmed kept him from returning to the big white house; however, their progress up the mountain was becoming slower and slower.

Maggie lay on her side, her knees pulled up, her head resting on her arm. Tingles in her arm brought her awake to find the light in their refuge dim. She sat up and looked across at Hadi. He sat, still upright, with his eyes closed. As she looked, he opened his eyes and smiled at her. The smile made Maggie feel appreciated and accepted. She felt loved in a special way, the way she used to feel when she was a little girl and her grandmother smiled at her. She smiled back gently and warmly.

"You are well rested, now, dear lady?" Hadi asked quietly.

"I am well rested, yes, Hadi," Maggie answered. "And you, are you rested also?"

"Oh, yes. I am rested. Soon we must be on our way. It will be best if we reach the road just after dark. Then we will be able to sneak across without detection," he said.

As they were talking the others stirred and were sitting up. "Shall we go? Are you ready?" asked Allie.

Andre and Brigitte nodded and stood up. "Let's go."

On their hands and knees one after the other they crawled out of the copse. There was more light outside. The sun was low on the horizon and cast a golden glow across the hillside. Hadi turned to the left and started walking, followed by the others. He led them on a course that paralleled the road above, but kept them out of sight of it.

Joe Morales and Sam Anderson topped the ridge gasping for breath. Turning, they looked back. There was Los Angeles, spread out below like a carpet. They watched the light become more golden as the sun sank lower in the west. Joe opened the binoculars and scanned the mountainside above them. For a moment he thought he caught a movement, but whatever it was, it was gone. Nothing. Just scrub growth and rocks. He felt the small telephone in his pocket. He and Harry had agreed not to use it unless there was real news.

Allie wondered how it was that Hadi knew the geography of this area; however, she had seen enough of his navigational skills that she no longer questioned his instincts. They continued around the mountain, climbing slowly and obliquely. In the lingering daylight, with the gradual ascent, the going was relatively easy and they made good time. In time they came to a dropping off place. The terrain dropped steeply into a canyon in which farther down they knew there were houses and civilization. It was tempting to go downhill, to try their luck in making their way to a telephone and help. But the stakes were high. Each of them knew that if they were recaptured there might not be another chance to escape. Additionally, each of them had developed a strong trust in Hadi and his ability to choose wisely for them.

They stood on the edge of the canyon for a while looking down. It already was dark in its depths. Resolutely Hadi turned uphill. As they followed the canyon's edge the light changed, going from golden to rosy, becoming darker and darker.

Allie stopped suddenly and said, "Listen. I hear cars." They stopped to listen. Above they could hear the sound of an occasional car.

"You have sharp ears, dear lady. We go quietly now, and slowly," Hadi said. After a few moments, they noticed the lights of the cars as they passed. Ahead loomed huge dark boulders. Thankfully, they sat in the shadows of the boulders. They could see the lights of the cars sweeping the boulders as they rounded a curve. They could hear the soft whoosh, whoosh as each car passed.

"Now is a time for caution. Now is a time for slow haste," Hadi said ambiguously. "This is a dangerous area for us, an area where we are most vulnerable. We will wait until it is truly dark. Then between cars we will hurry across the road. But we need to know where we are going once we are on the other side. That side of the road does not have as many boulders as this one. One of us needs to cross first and find a secluded resting spot on the other side."

Maggie thought for a moment and said, "Hadi, could Allie and I both cross and find a spot. Then together we can direct the others to safety?"

He answered, "Excellent. But you must go quickly and quietly. You must become as little mice in the night. Allah is with us. We are protected. But we do not want to put Allah to too much trouble!"

Allie and Maggie crouched and crawled over the rocks. Not for the first time, Maggie was grateful that she was wearing jeans and a dark sweater and walking shoes. Allie was dressed similarly. In addition each wore her shoulder bag across one shoulder. Allie wore one of the canteens across the other shoulder. They poked their heads above the rocks and looked down at the road. From this vantage they could see it winding away in both directions, following the crest of the ridge. The lights of an approaching car became brighter and brighter, illuminating the sides of the road. Suddenly, Allie reached over and shoved her mother's head down as she, herself, ducked behind the rock. Light passed over their heads and lighted the rocks behind them. Maggie drew in her breath. The light passed on and illumined both sides of the road farther down.

"Yeah, real close. That was a spotlight. They're still looking. Rats!" Allie said. "Hadi was right. This is a very dangerous place. I'm beginning to feel like little Eva. Thank God they haven't thought of using dogs!"

Maggie shivered. "Right," she said. Far off, to the left, they could see more lights approaching.

"Mom, we need to dash for it as soon as this next car passes. I'll lead, you follow me. Okay?" Allie said.

"Okay," answered Maggie, wondering just where they would dash to and hoping there was a sheltered spot somewhere on the other side. The car came closer, lights scouring the roadside. Again they ducked behind the rock. As soon as the lights had disappeared around the bend, Allie rose, motioned to Maggie and scrambled down to the road. Maggie followed. They went without speaking, bending low, running. On the other side of the road, they searched first up the road and then down. There was no decent cover anywhere, only short, dry grass and rocky soil, but straight ahead the ground dropped off slightly.

"This has to be it," Allie said, "We just have to get them over here. They can . . . .." She broke off as another set of headlights and the dangerous spotlights approached. "Quick, Mom. Lie down—flat!" She whispered. They flattened themselves on the ground just as the spotlight swept over their heads.

"Whew! Close again," Maggie said. "There're so many of them. They must think we're very important." Just then a car came by slowly. No spotlights this time, just driving by slowly.

When it had passed Allie said, "Now, here's what I want you to do. I'll cross back over and send the others to you. You meet them at the side of the road, lead them over here and make sure they lie down. Okay? And, Mom? Be sure to keep your head down."

"Yes, I will," Maggie answered. After the next searching car passed, Allie ran across the road and disappeared behind the rocks. After the next car, Maggie ran up to the road to meet Brigitte and Hadi running her way. Quickly, she led them away from the road to where the land dropped off. They had just hit the ground when they saw more lights approaching. Maggie reached over and pushed both heads to the ground. She had started back to the road when Andre and Allie appeared, running, bending low. Together they joined Hadi and Brigitte, lying just below the crest of the ridge.

"Now what?" asked Andre, speaking for all of them.

"Now, my dear friends, we walk. We walk away from this dangerous spot to find sanctuary," replied Hadi.

Maggie's heart sank at this. They were so close here. If only the cars and their dreaded spotlights would go away surely they could find help right on this road. She hadn't yet forgotten her fatigue of yesterday. Her body reminded her with sore and stiff muscles every time she moved.

Hadi said, "It is true that this seems to be an oasis in the desert, but we must remember that not everything is as it seems. It is important to follow Hadi without question to the true resting place."

Maggie thought about what seemed to be an uncanny ability of Hadi's to sense her thoughts and feelings. She also remembered that so far, they had avoided capture. She sighed and said, "Well, Hadi, let's get going. I'm looking forward to that true oasis."

They moved away from the road, at first on hands and knees and then upright, single file behind Hadi. No one spoke. Each one was locked into his or her own thoughts. They went downhill at first, away from the road. When they were well out of sight of the road, Hadi led them on a diagonal route ever north. The partial moon gave little illumination. It was difficult to see where they were heading, yet Hadi moved forward confidently and sure-footedly, as if he were strolling along a boulevard.

They alternately climbed and then descended, but they seemed to be avoiding the sharp scrambles of last night. Maggie felt grateful that they were not climbing and descending steep inclines. The muscles in her legs were sore and she felt each up and down step more than the level ones. They had walked, almost leisurely, for a couple of hours when Hadi stopped for a rest in an area of large stones. They sat down thankfully. Hadi doled out trail mix to each person and then passed the water bottle. It was the last of the water from their prison. Water had never tasted so good. Maggie thought that it seemed like a lifetime since she had crawled out through the tiny high window and they had escaped.

The Ferret and Bruno scrambled up the mountain in the dark. Ferret guided their progress by the huge sign above them. The night was dark and it was difficult to see where they were going. He thought once again of returning to the big white house, but the thought of Ahmed discouraged him. He could not imagine how they could find their prisoners in the dark on this huge mountainside. Behind him he could hear Bruno mumbling curses in Arabic. Bruno's mood was becoming ever blacker. Maybe the prisoners had been found already and he and Bruno were enduring this torture for nothing.

Harry Cavanaugh sat in his car at the scenic overlook. Below him were the lights of the Los Angeles Basin as far as his eyes could see. He knew there was little he could do from here, but even so, he wanted to be up here just in case. If word should come that the McGill women had been found this might be a better place for him to be. The night was black and he wondered where they were and what was happening to them. Were they on this mountain? Were they alone? WHO was with them? These were not happy thoughts. Harry stretched his neck, trying to ease the stiffness in it. Beside him, the telephone remained silent. He poured another cup of coffee from the thermos and sighed.

The night remained quite dark. The stars shone brightly in the inky sky. The horizons held yellow glows from the city that they knew was all around them. Yet here, there was quiet. Here they felt away from the civilized, mechanized world. In the distance they could hear a dog barking.

"It's a beautiful night," Maggie observed.

"This would be almost fun under different circumstances," Allie said.

Hadi drew in a long breath and said, "But, dear lady, this is just what it is. Can we not enjoy what is enjoyable? We are here. It is beautiful, yes? Let us praise Allah for what is beautiful, for what is pleasurable in the moment. After all, our lives are only moments strung together, like beads on a thread. Let us be happy for the beautiful beads. If there are others, we will address them when they arrive."

There was a silence as the little group pondered this observation. A chill little breeze blew against Maggie's face. She had not noticed the coolness while they were walking. The dog still was barking. It seemed as if the barking was closer than before.

After a while Andre spoke, "*Oui,* Hadi, it is true. We do have only moments. And this moment, here under the stars with good friends. This is a good moment. *Oui*, a good moment." He put an arm around Brigitte and held her close, murmuring to her in French.

As one, the little band rose and resumed their trek. When they stopped for the next rest the slivered moon was low on the western horizon. To their left they could see the bulk of the large mountain they had been skirting. One and all they were happy not to have attempted climbing such a huge slope.

They continued. One foot in front of the other. Maggie lost track of time. It seemed as if she had been walking for her whole life. Now they were moving more steeply downhill. From time to time there were glimpses of lights far ahead of them. Occasionally they would cross a ravine, a steep washed out area with heavier vegetation. The climb down brought screams of protest from her already sore muscles. Each climb up left her out of breath.

Resting after one such climb, Maggie became aware of a dog barking somewhere near. In the dim moonlight she looked at the others. Surely their pursuers would not bring dogs to track them. Allie had heard the barking too and clutched Maggie's hand.

Hadi saw their clenched hands and spoke, "Please do not alarm yourselves, dear ones. If there were dogs tracking us, we would hear more than one bark. This is only one dog. He has been with us for a while. He barks only when we stop, have you not noticed?"

As Hadi stopped speaking there was a rustling in the ravine behind them. A small whitish creature careened out of the bushes and flung itself toward Allie. It stopped at her feet, wagged a tail, licked her hand and lay down.

Allie exclaimed, "Oh, look, Mom! Hadi!" Then to the creature, "Where'd you come from? Who are you? How'd you find us?" She bent down and scratched him behind the ears. The tail beat a hard tattoo on the dry ground. He rolled over, then jumped up and with great dignity ceremoniously greeted each person in turn, returning to lie at Allie's feet.

Maggie laughed, "Well, Allie, I don't know who he is or where he came from, but I do believe he thinks he belongs to you!"

Allie laughed in return, "So it would seem." She stood up. "Well, come on then, Dog. Let's get on with it." They all stood up and started walking. The little dog trotted along beside Allie, occasionally running ahead to Hadi, as if he were checking out their route. The going was easier now. Below the lights of the city could be seen. Maggie began to notice a lightening of the eastern sky. She looked up. The stars were beginning to fade. Soon it would be light. Morning again. She wondered where they were.

The progress of the little band had become slower and slower as the night wore on. Brigitte had made a valiant effort to keep up with the group and they, in turn, had adjusted their pace to accommodate her. Their stops for rest had were coming more frequently and each one lasted longer. Now Brigitte had slowed noticeably and Andre was supporting her, half carrying her. Hadi signaled that they stop once again to rest.

The telephone beside him beeped discreetly. Harry's head jerked. He grabbed the phone before his eyes were open, "Yes?"

"Harry, where are you? I've got something to tell you. I don't want to say it on this phone." The voice was tired, but held a note of excitement.

138

"Yeah, Okay, Carlos. You at the office?" Harry asked. He looked around, surprised to see dawn approaching. The sky was becoming lighter by the moment.

"Right. Harry, don't get too excited. It's not much, but might be something."

"Right now I'll take anything. I'll call you back soon." Harry put the phone down, started his car, turned around and drove off in search of a phone booth.

The morning gray brightened as the sun approached the horizon. From her rock Maggie looked around at her companions. Hadi looked scarcely the worse for his trip, almost as if he had been out for a Sunday stroll. The stress of his concern for Brigitte and the physical ordeal showed in Andre's shadowed eyes and the slump of his shoulders. Allie, too, looked spent and tired. Even so, Maggie thought she looked beautiful with her blond hair in disarray and the color that exercise had brought to her face. Brigitte seemed to be completely exhausted. Her face was pale as she leaned against Andre's shoulder with her eyes closed.

Maggie met Hadi's eyes. She wondered what he saw. There was silent acknowledgment of their situation in his look. He said, "We have come a very long way. It was a successful night. We even found a new friend." He smiled at Dog. "We have earned food and rest." So saying, he opened the pack he carried on his shoulder and passed around half sandwiches. Carefully, he cut two apples in half and passed these around also, bypassing himself. Loudly, he said, *"Enchallah!"*

In unison the others echoed, *"Enchallah!"* And they ate.

Hadi took the small thermos from the pack and slowly poured still hot coffee into the plastic cap. This he carried to Brigitte and held for her while she sipped it. When she had finished, he said, "There's another cup of coffee left. Would anyone care for a few sips?"

They looked at one another. Maggie shook her head and said, "I'm not a coffee drinker, Hadi. But thank you very much."

Allie said, "Why don't we save what's left. I feel much better after eating and I don't think I need it right now. We may need it more later."

Andre held Brigitte and nodded his head in agreement. Brigitte seemed to have perked up. Food and the hot coffee clearly had improved her energy level.

Allie unstrapped the canteen from her shoulder and passed it around the circle. They each sipped the water sparingly. Maggie considered the incongruity of their situation. They were in the midst of one of the largest cities in the world and yet they were in a wilderness.

As they rested, the sun rose over the eastern horizon. Suddenly, Allie laughed out loud. Her laughter rang in the quiet morning air. Maggie looked at her in alarm. Whatever was so funny?

She continued laughing, then picked up the little dog and laughed some more. "Look, Mom! Look! Look who he is. He's a Jack Russell! Can you believe it? A Jack Russell!"

Maggie looked at the little dog and joined her laughter. The others were puzzled by their merriment. After Allie explained her dream of God speaking to her, Andre and Brigitte joined them with chuckled with them. Hadi just smiled.

It had been a long night for Ahmed. When the Hollywood house became unavailable he continued to direct the search from a small house in the Valley. The escape of all their prisoners was catastrophic. They must be found. He had expected they would be discovered on the road through the mountains. But now morning had arrived. He sat at a table alone, his head in his hands. One of the phones rang.

"Yes?"

The voice did not need to identify itself. "There is nothing. The prisoners have disappeared. There are more police up on the mountain. We had to leave. What next?"

Ahmed reached for a large-scale map of the Griffith Park area. "If they still are out there, they may have gone even farther north. Let's check out the north side of the park. It would not be a logical choice for them, but they have avoided the obvious so far." He put the phone down, stood up and started pacing.

Carlos picked up the phone on the first ring, "Yeah?"

"What's up?" Harry asked.

"Well, I told you not to get excited. But, it's kind of interesting. Yesterday afternoon two bicyclists reported having their food and water stolen up on Mt. Lee. They'd hidden their bikes behind some rocks and walked across the road. They were gone about fifteen minutes. When they got back all their food and water were gone. They had money and cameras in their bags. But the only stuff taken was food and water. They said there was no sign of any other people up there during that time. No cars, no other cyclists." Carlos' voice was low and non-committal, but it held a hint of excitement.

"This happened yesterday afternoon?" Harry questioned.

"Yeah, about one o'clock, they said."

"Why did it take us this long to hear about it?"

"They didn't report it until they got home last night. Nobody thought much about it. I only just got it because someone I know over there knows we're working the area right now," Carlos explained.

"Well, you're right. On the face of it, it doesn't sound like much. But it's puzzling. Clearly, someone wanted food and water enough to steal it. It wasn't an ordinary theft. The obvious stuff wasn't taken. Do you think our ladies have taken up petty thievery? But if they made it to the road, why didn't they just walk down and find help?" Harry puzzled.

"That brings us to the next thing," Carlos said. "There was an unusual amount of traffic up there last night. A patrol car stopped a vehicle that was driving slowly up and down with spotlights searching the sides of the road. Now get this. It was driven by a guy wearing a turban and his address was the same as the white house. And there was more than one car. They said there were looking for a valuable dog."

"Some dog!" Harry said. "But you know, this is good news. If they were looking, that means our ladies may be on the loose. Now, if those women made it that far and they couldn't use the road, where do you suppose they went?"

"There aren't many easy choices up there. They might be hiding somewhere near the road. Maybe they took off overland again," Carlos ventured.

"What happened to the cars with the lights? I was up there early this morning and I didn't see anything like that," Harry said.

"Well, that patrolman told them to go home and give the wildlife a chance!" Carlos chuckled.

"Carlos, can we get some people up there to nose around the area where the bicyclists were robbed? See if we can find anything. I know it's a long shot, but let's try," Harry said, feeling more hopeful than he had since Maggie's call had been interrupted.

"Okay, Harry. You got it," said Carlos.

Chapter Twelve

They relaxed for an hour more, stretching out on the sandy ground, watching the sun rise higher in the sky. Maggie dozed for a few moments. With food and rest, their mood lightened. Daylight showed them to be within easy walking distance of civilization. It seemed as if their troubles were over. At last, Hadi's "true oasis" was within sight. When she roused and stood up, Maggie had an impulse to run full tilt down the mountain into a house or business and ask for sanctuary.

Hadi smiled and said, "Ah, dear ones, it does appear as if we have found what we have been seeking. But, let us proceed always with caution. We now will be crossing a boundary, out of the wilderness that has been our safety, into civilization that can be a wilderness in itself. Let us go." They rose and continued down the mountain, picking their way around scrub growth of sage and chaparral, their hearts light in spite of Hadi's warning. In the distance, Maggie could see what appeared to be an open grassy area with trees. It looked like a park of some kind. All it lacked to be a true oasis was a fountain of water. They walked on, coming ever closer to their goal.

Maggie narrowed her eyes and peered expectantly. "Oh, my God," she gasped.

Simultaneously Allie said, "Jeez!"

"It's a cemetery," Andre muttered.

"It must be Forest Lawn," Allie said.

As they came nearer the grave markers became clear. Sprinklers flowed. The fountains of their oasis. The grass was lush and neatly manicured. Dog danced at their feet, running ahead to check on Hadi's leadership and then back to prance at Allie's feet. After their adventure, crossing the enclosing fence was simple. They handed the little dog across. The moment he was on the bright green grass, he streaked off as fast as his short legs would carry him. Maggie watched him go and wondered if their brief and intense relationship was over. Was he deserting them?

Once inside, they sat down in the soft green grass under the shade of a spreading gray-green olive tree. There was the very civilized smell of newly mown grass. In the distance they could hear the gentle putt-putt sound of sprinklers in motion. Hadi passed the canteen and each one drank thankfully. Maggie looked around at her companions. Each face showed the relief they were feeling. They had crossed the "desert". They had found their oasis. Now, rescue was at hand. They had only to walk through the cemetery until they found help. Maggie was surprised that she was feeling somehow let down, almost sad. It was only then that she realized how much she valued the bond that had been created among these four people with whom she had shared the ordeal of imprisonment, danger and hardship.

Maggie spoke, "You know, this whole thing is almost over. We'll be rescued. The authorities will take over and we'll be safe. Probably we'll separate and we might not ever see each other again. I just want you to know that I feel close to each of you and I don't want us to lose the bond that's grown between us." She stopped for a moment, looked down at the ground and frowned. Then she continued, "I'm not saying this very well. But, in a funny sort of way, this has been a very special experience. I think what I'll remember about this time is not so much the danger and the hardship, but rather how close I feel to each of you and how much I value the closeness." She stopped, feeling a little embarrassed.

There was a long silence. Andre broke the silence, "*Oui*, Maggie. I understand what you are saying. I, too, feel that. We are five separate people who have been put together by fate in this difficult situation. Now, it feels as if we have become a little family. *Oui*. It is good to be so."

Hadi glowed beneficently at them in the ensuing silence. He said, "It is true that we have become a family. It is true that we have experienced our oneness with one another. It is true that we also are one with Allah. This we have felt through our ordeal. We have felt our oneness with Allah and with all that is. It is good."

Allie said thoughtfully, "I guess if we're one with one another then we never can be separated, even if we should not see one another again."

Hadi looked at her tenderly and said, "Yes, dear lady. That is so. And if that is so, then we do not need to grieve a separation. Is that not so?"

Allie returned his look and nodded.

They sat thoughtfully for a while. Then Hadi spoke again, "Our experience together has had many flavors. We have tasted despair, hardship, fatigue, pain, and fear. We also have tasted loyalty, truth, goodness, strength, understanding, and love. It is good to remember that the same experience has brought many things, things that we could call both good and bad. If we had not been brought together in this way, we would have missed the opportunity to taste these particular flavors."

Maggie's heart felt very full and there was a tightness in her throat. For a moment she felt almost grateful for the last forty-eight hours. She looked around the circle and saw her feelings mirrored in the faces there. There was no need for words. They sat for a few more minutes and then slowly, helping one another to their feet, they rose and in a body, walked down the grassy slope, looking for the world they had left for a while.

The sun was warm on her shoulders and Maggie thought that the sun was shining in her heart, also. The cemetery was quiet, birds sang overhead, the sky was blue. It was a lovely morning. Maggie's sore and aching muscles seemed to be complaining less. They came upon a paved road and started down it. As they reached the brow of a hill, they looked down on a gathering of people and cars. A funeral. Maggie wondered what the protocol of such a situation was. Simply to walk up in a body and announce their plight seemed intrusive and insensitive to the feelings of the mourners. Hadi must have had similar sensitivities because he motioned that they stand behind a large headstone and wait for the service to come to an end

After checking out the course of the funeral, Allie plopped down on the grass and leaned against a headstone. The others followed her lead. The sun against the stone created a soothingly warm spot and Maggie felt her eyes closing. She was drifting down into a warm peaceful place, her body relaxing in soft little stages.

The peace of her nap was shattered by furious barking and a hard, wet little body flinging itself across her body toward

Allie. Maggie jerked herself awake, blinked her eyes and looked around. Her companions were in similar states of shock and surprise. Beyond them, around the curves of the drive, came a large black car. Maggie shook her head in disbelief. They couldn't be here! Not here in this peaceful setting! Not when safety was so near. The occupants of the car must have seen them because it picked up speed and was racing toward them.

Allie grabbed Maggie's arm and shouted, "COME ON! Let's get out of here." Maggie started running as fast as her legs would go. Around her the others were also running. Running. Running between the headstones, down the hill toward the solemn ceremony. Below and ahead of them heads jerked up, staring in shock at the spectacle of the newcomers. They saw five disheveled and apparently deranged people shouting and running headlong toward them, accompanied by a compact, furiously barking dog.

The mourners scattered as the runners approached. Below them, parked at the edge of the road were limos, cars, a florist's van and the hearse.

Maggie's breath was coming in gasps. Could they make it before the black car caught them? Hurry. Faster, faster. It was a nightmare come true. Things seemed to be happening in slow motion. Her legs seemed to move so slowly. Around her the others were moving slowly, slowly. What about the car. Was it going slowly also?

Allie noticing her mother's distress, grabbed her hand and pulled her along. A quick glance showed her that Andre was pulling Brigitte in the same way. Hadi was moving very fast, but apparently effortlessly. They were approaching the open grave. The mourners now were running, as well, for their cars or simply to hide behind trees and stones. A dark green canvas canopy shaded the grave and the surrounding folding chairs. To the side stood the metal trolley that had carried the casket. It seemed that the little band was thinking as a group. Allie pushed her mother onto the trolley. Andre put Brigitte on the other side. The two women crouched on its steel rails while the other three pushed it pell-mell down the hill toward the vehicles.

The black car had been unable to follow them directly because of the headstones. It was circling along the drive. It would be here any moment. To Maggie, clinging to the trolley as it bounced down the hill, it seemed as if they were flying. Cars lined the road in front of them. Hadi directed them between two parked cars heading toward the florist's van. There was a crash! Maggie wasn't sure what had happened. There was a flash of bright yellow. She and Brigitte and Andre were in a heap of bodies in the middle of the road. The trolley careened down the road freed of its passengers. Allie was sprawled across an identified body in bright yellow running shorts. Hadi miraculously stayed upright and was pulling them to their feet.

"Hurry. Hurry. Get up. Get up fast!" Hadi was urging.

Somehow, they sorted themselves out and piled into the back of the flower van. Allie jumped into the driver's seat, said a prayer of thanksgiving that the keys were in the ignition. The engine jumped to life and they pulled out into the road just as the black car rounded the curve behind them.

Maggie looked out the back window to see outraged mourners racing down to the road, a wrathful van driver waving his arms, a shocked clergyman in black. The graveside was a shambles of overturned chairs and a lopsided canopy. To her dismay, the black car was much too near. Then the van swayed sharply and she was thrown across it into Andre's arms. Dog yelped sharply as she stepped on his foot. She pulled herself up and looked back again. The black car had crashed into the abandoned trolley and its windshield had been shattered. A turbaned figure was pulling the twisted trolley away from the black car.

"Did you see that, Allie?" Maggie shouted.

"Yeah, hooray!" Allie answered.

"Who exactly are you people? What are you doing? And where the hell are we going?" Asked a querulous voice from a dark corner of the van.

Maggie's head jerked up in surprise. She squinted into the corner toward the voice. Long tan legs unfolded under bright yellow shorts. Holding on the sides of the jolting van, the bent legs moved forward to disclose the muscular upper torso of the unlucky runner. Short light brown wavy hair above a tanned chiseled face and brilliant blue eyes. Maggie gasped as she recognized the runner from the Malibu beach of a few days ago. "You! Who are you? And what are you doing here?"

Allie glanced around briefly to look at the newcomer. She recognized him immediately. He was memorable. She echoed her mother, "YOU! Who are you? What in the world are you doing here?"

The startled runner looked from one of the women to the other. "Who am *I*? No. No. Who are you? I asked first." He stopped for a moment. "Wait a minute. Do I know you? No. Impossible. If I knew anyone as madcap as you people, I'd remember."

Hadi, Andre and Brigitte observed this interchange silently.

"Madcap! Madcap!" Allie's voice rose in outrage, the frustration of the past few days flowing out in the two words. "I, I. . . You! You! . .," she sputtered. She closed her mouth tightly and concentrated on driving.

The runner looked helplessly at the others. "Could someone please explain just what's going down here? I was just out for a morning run when your chariot ran me down. I'm not sure how I happened to get in here with you nuts."

Maggie stared at him, her mouth slightly open. Brigitte leaned against Andre in the corner, scarcely raising her head to look at the runner.

Hadi gazed at him with a smile and finally said, "Allow me to introduce us. Me. My name is Mohammed Hadi El Kabir. You may call me Hadi. I am at your service, dear sir, and I will answer any questions I can. In the corner are Monsieur and Madame Fouchet."

Andre extended his hand and said, "How do you do. Please. Please call us Andre and Brigitte." Brigitte raised her head and smiled faintly.

Hadi turned to Maggie. "This dear lady is Maggie McGill who has come to California to visit her daughter. Our driver is Miss Allie McGill."

Maggie nodded at the runner. Allie made no acknowledgment of the introduction.

Hadi continued, "May I inquire your name, dear sir?"

Yellow shorts replied in a calmer voice, "My name is Maximillian LaCroix. My friends call me Max. It certainly has been interesting meeting you. But can you tell me what we're doing now? Are you grave robbers? Or what? Why was that black car chasing you?"

Hadi replied, "The answer to that is a long story. May I just say that we each were abducted by some unpleasant people who imprisoned us against our wills. At the proper time we escaped our prison and so far we have been successful in eluding recapture. Eluding recapture is where we are at this moment. It is interesting that Allah has chosen to place you in our midst, is it not?"

Max considered this last and said, "I'm not sure that I want to burden Allah with the responsibility for my being run down by a reckless casket trolley! Who abducted you and why? I know there must be more to this story than that."

Allie, who had been listening from the driver's seat, called out. "Does anyone back there know this area? I need a navigator to get me out of here."

Max crawled to the front and took the passenger's seat. "I come up here from time to time if I'm in the neighborhood. It makes a new place to run. Actually, you could drop me at my car. It's not far from here."

Allie gave him an astonished look. "You must be kidding. We're running to save our lives and you want to be dropped at your car!"

Max looked at her sheepishly and said, "I'm sorry. You know, the idea of your running for your lives on such a lovely morning is hard for me to take in. It seems unreal. How can I help you?"

As she swung the van around a curve, Allie glanced at him and spoke more gently, "We need to put as much space between us and this place as quickly as possible. They had a telephone and probably have other cars heading for us right now. Guide me out of here."

"Okay. That I can do. Turn right here. Good." As Max continued giving Allie instructions, he stared at her profile. "I know this sounds like an old line, but I'm sure I know you from somewhere. I just can't remember where."

Allie smiled and concentrated on her driving. The little Jack Russell had made his way to the front of the van and sat between Allie and Max, his tongue lolling out of the side of his mouth, a happy look on his face. Allie reached down and patted the top of his head.

"Thank you, little dog, for alerting us. If it weren't for you, we'd have been caught for sure," she said. Dog thumped his tail to say *you're welcome.*

They left the cemetery and turned on to a road leading toward a freeway. Allie turned her head and said, "Hadi, I'm sure they had a telephone in their car. I'd think that they'll be after us soon. This van isn't going to be safe. What'll we do?"

Hadi thought for a moment and said, "The problem, of course, is that our escape then becomes a trap. Even if we leave it, this vehicle still could lead the others to us. This is, indeed, an interesting problem."

Maggie said, "It seems to me that once we find a telephone, we probably don't need to avoid them for very long. Why don't we just find a congested shopping center or supermarket, park the van among others, run to the store, call Harry and wait."

There was a short silence. Then Allie said, "Of course. That's the answer. Do you all agree?"

Max answered, "It seems like a plan to me."

The others nodded their agreement.

Allie turned the van under the freeway and headed in the direction that seemed most congested. They drove down a wide street lined with automobile dealerships, convenience stores, and fast food restaurants. Suddenly she swerved the van sharply into a used car lot, drove toward the rear and parked it among several other vans.

"Okay, everyone. This is where we walk again. But not far this time. Next door is a burger place. Let's stroll over, give Harry Cavanaugh a call, and have something to eat. I'll treat!" Allie's voice was triumphant. With a big grin, she dropped the van's keys in the ashtray and walked around to the rear to help the others disembark. One by one, out they came. Tired, disheveled and very happy.

Allie picked Dog up and carried him under her arm as they walked cautiously between the cars, crossed the parking lot and entered the burger restaurant. After setting Dog at the door Allie walked immediately to the rear and a telephone. She dropped a quarter in, dialed the number that she was sure she'd never forget and listened.

"Cavanaugh," said a tired voice.

"Hello, Mr. Cavanaugh. This is Allie McGill."

Before she could say another word, Harry shouted, "Allie? You're okay? Where are you? How's your mother? Where've you been? We've been worried. . . ."

Allie cut in with a laugh, "Wait, wait. One at a time. Yes, I'm okay and so is Mom. We're at a Burger Delight in Burbank. Would you like to send taxi service?"

"Would I ever! You just stay put and out of sight. I'll be there in fifteen minutes. But I'll see if I can get someone else there sooner. What's the address?" Harry's voice was light with relief.

Allie gave him the address and said, "Send something big enough for six. Our numbers have grown!"

Harry said, "Right. Will do. See you soon."

Harry walked to the outer office and speaking rapidly, said, "Pete, I'm going to pick up the McGill women." He gave Pete the address. "Get on the scrambler and see if we have anyone near there who can be there sooner. Oh, and give me the keys to that limo."

Pete raised his eyebrows and tossed the keys to Harry. Now, what has him in such a tizzy?

Allie found Maggie and Brigitte in the Ladies Room, splashing water on their faces, taking turns using Maggie's comb and spare lipstick. Allie looked in the large mirror and laughed. Maggie met her eyes and laughed with her. With a glance in the mirror, Brigitte joined their merriment. What they saw was comical. Three wild looking women with their hair in all directions, the water had only made muddy streaks on their sunburned faces. Hastily applied lipstick gave them a clownish impression. Helping each other, they did as much as they could for their appearance.

Andre, Hadi and Max were ordering sandwiches, French fries and drinks when they came out. The restaurant employees seemed not even to notice the unkempt appearance of these customers. California, Maggie thought. Nothing surprises Californians.

Harry made the trip to the Burger Delight in just less than seventeen minutes. He found the little band of travelers respectfully silent as they wolfed down their food. As he approached the table, Maggie and Allie jumped up and spontaneously greeted him with big hugs. Harry stood a little stiffly at first, not quite sure how to respond, but then he relaxed and returned their hugs. Maggie performed the introductions and pulled up an extra chair for Harry.

They offered him food, but Harry settled for a cup of coffee. While they ate, they began to fill him in on their adventures.

"Harry, we're grateful for your help and rescue. Thank you for coming so quickly," Maggie said.

"You're more welcome than you know, Maggie," was Harry's response. He smiled at her, crinkles forming around his eyes.

Maggie smiled back and thought he didn't look quite as tired as she remembered. She leaned back in her chair and looked around. The brightness and slickness of the restaurant seemed somehow strange and foreign to her. She wondered if she'd soon become re-accustomed to this urban world, or if she always would feel slightly estranged from it as she did now.

When they all finished eating, Harry said, "I'd like to offer you a place to stay until we've cleared up this situation. We have a safe house where you may stay for as long as it takes. Let's get going."

Any place that provided safety and hot running water sounded like heaven to Maggie. A look at the other faces told her that they felt the same.

Max stood up and said, "Since I only recently have joined this group, I don't need the safe house. I'd like to stick around for a while and find out what happens next though."

Allie looked up at him and smiled, "Max, it's been nice seeing you again."

He gave her a puzzled look, a little frown between his eyes. "You see, I think I do know you from somewhere. But I think if we'd met, I wouldn't have forgotten. Obviously you remember. Won't you tell me?" He thought for a moment and then turning to Harry said, "Harry, if someone would drop me at my car, I'd like to go with my friends."

Harry looked at him, and then glanced around the group, almost as if he were asking their feelings about this request. "I'm sorry," Harry said, looking from Max to Allie and back again, "but that would be strictly against policy. With any luck we'll wind this whole thing up in a day or two and your friends will be free. Then everything'll be back to normal. Pete Corelli is outside in that blue car. He'll take you back to your automobile."

At this, Maggie laughed to herself. What would a 'normal' life be like? She felt that she'd never had such an experience. But she understood what Harry was saying. Costa Mira and her counseling practice were somewhere in the recesses of her consciousness, a dim memory, a little like a dream one only just remembers. What would it be like to go back there now? Surely she wouldn't be the same person who'd left it only a few days ago.

Max nodded his head reluctantly and acquiesced. To Allie he said, "Please give me your phone number and I'll give you mine. Let's talk as soon as you're free. How about dinner on your first night back?"

"Sure, okay" Allie answered and gave him her number.

Harry pulled the limo up to the side door of the Burger Delight and hurried the five refugees into its depths. Dog jumped in with them. They were mostly silent as the limousine carried them smoothly and elegantly to their new resting place. Out the window Maggie saw a quiet winding residential street, lush with shrubbery and lined with tall palm trees. The houses were set well back from the street behind tall fences. At the gated driveway, Harry spoke to the electronic box and the gate swung open silently. The limo circled to the side of the house and into a garage. When the garage door had closed, Harry opened the car's doors and invited them into the house. Maggie had a momentary *deja vu*, remembering the garage at the white house, and she said a silent 'thank you' to be here and not there.

Harry led them into a living room comfortably furnished with soft deep sofas and chairs grouped around a fireplace. "Make yourselves at home. We have a small staff here. They'll be happy to get you anything you need. You have the run of the house, but please stay indoors."

Harry turned as a tall, muscular man entered the living room. "Oh, good. This is Fritz. He'll do his best to make you comfortable and to keep you safe. He's the boss here. So pay attention and let him run things."

Fritz turned to them and smiled a broad lopsided smile. "Welcome to our little place. Right now, you're the most important people in my life. Like Harry said, we have a few rules, so I guess it's best to get those straight right away. The first is that you stay indoors all the time. Second, no telephone calls. If you must get a message to someone out there, let me know and I'll see that the message is relayed. Third, try to imagine this is a spa and enjoy yourselves. The kitchen is open any time. We'll be serving meals at regular hours. If you have any dietary requests, just let us know. There are radios and televisions in each bedroom as well as a large screen set here and in the library. The library, by the way, is well stocked. On the lower level there's a fully equipped workout room and a sauna. Mildred'll be around to help you find clean clothes from our wardrobe. Now, if you'll follow me I'll show you to your rooms."

From the living room, Fritz led them into a large hall and up a short flight of stairs. Here, he assigned Maggie and Allie to adjoining rooms connected by a shared bath. Andre and Brigitte were given a room across from Maggie's and Hadi was in a room next to theirs.

After inspecting their rooms, Maggie flopped down on one of the twin beds in her room. In a few minutes Allie wandered in, lay down on the next bed and said, "Mom, I know it may be silly, but would it be all right with you if I slept in here tonight? I just sort of want to stay close. Is that okay?"

Maggie looked at her with tears in her eyes. "Oh, honey. Of course, it is. It's more than okay. It's just what I was thinking myself." Then changing the subject, "How about a bath? Who goes first?"

"Didn't you notice, Mom? There's a shower and a tub. We can bathe at the same time. Which do you want?"

Maggie chose the shower. It was one of the most memorable showers of her life. Long, leisurely, hot and steamy. When she emerged, Allie was wrapped in a huge terry robe.

Allie said, "Now, I am going to try that shower. The bath was good, but I'm going for the whole thing." So saying, she stepped into the shower. Maggie found a second terry robe on the back of the bathroom door. Wrapped in the robe, she blew her hair dry and wondered what would happen next. Would they go home tomorrow?

Chapter Thirteen

Smooth sheets, soft pillow, blissful silence, a feeling of cleanliness and peace. Maggie opened her eyes to find the room in soft early morning light. In the bed next to hers Allie stretched and rolled over, still sleeping peacefully. Dog lay asleep at the foot of Allie's bed. Maggie looked around the dimly lit room. A spacious, homey room furnished with dark traditional furniture and soft pastel colors. Very restful. Maggie grinned to herself when she realized that she and Allie had slept through dinner last night. What had caused her to wake was a gnawing feeling in her stomach and from somewhere below the faint aroma of coffee brewing and bacon frying. "Yummy!" she sighed.

At this Allie rolled, stretched again and opened her eyes. "Hi, Mom. What's up?"

"Well, I'm soon to be! I'm famished!" Maggie answered and swung her legs over the side of the bed.

"What time is it?" Allie asked.

"I'm not sure, but early morning, I think. We must've slept a very long time," Maggie answered. "How're you feeling?"

Allie became vertical, stretched again and took a few tentative steps. "Aside from being a little stiff and sore and very hungry, I think I feel absolutely fine," she said.

Maggie brushed her teeth and splashed water on her face at one of the twin lavatories. Next to her Allie did the same. Their clothes from last night had disappeared. Laid across the chaise lounge in the corner, Maggie found pale blue cotton slacks and shirt that fit perfectly after she rolled up the slacks' legs. She slipped into the soft leather moccasins she found with the clothes and walked into Allie's room.

"Oh, good. You're ready. Let's find that food!" Allie said as she zipped her slacks and stepped into sandals. Dog followed them downstairs, wagging his tail, as if he had a happy grin on his whiskered face.

In the dining room they met the Fouchets and Hadi seated at one end of a long mahogany table. They were sipping coffee and tea and chatting quietly. Maggie and Allie helped themselves to tea and fruit from the sideboard and sat down.

"Ah, good morning dear ladies. Did you sleep well?" Hadi asked with a mischievous twinkle. "Is this not a true oasis?"

"Yes, Hadi, we did sleep well. In fact, we must've slept twelve or fourteen hours nonstop. How about you? Andre and Brigitte? Did you all sleep well also?" Maggie asked. As she formed the question she looked at her friends. Hadi looked rested and relaxed, but then, he rarely looked tired or stressed. Andre and Brigitte both looked rested and happy.

Hadi nodded in response to her question and Andre said, "Oh, yes, thank you. We slept well. We both feel much better." He looked at Brigitte and smiled protectively.

Brigitte looked first at Andre and then said to Maggie, "*Oui, oui.* It is better now, no? I sleep well. I am feeling very well. Yes."

Just then Fritz entered and inquired what Maggie and Allie would like for breakfast. The five refugees chatted until their breakfasts arrived a few minutes later. After a hearty *'Enchallah'* in unison, a silence descended as they respectfully enjoyed their breakfasts. Even Hadi ate gustily. While they were eating Mildred entered with a plate of food for Dog that she placed on the floor in the corner of the room.

They had just started on second cups of coffee and tea when Harry Cavanaugh and John Landis entered the dining room. Harry and John helped themselves to coffee and Harry introduced John to everyone except Andre. Andre and John greeted one another heartily.

Harry looked at them and smiled. "Well, good news for you all. During the night we rounded up and arrested Ahmed and thirty-seven others from his organization. We're looking for a few others. With cooperation from you five we should be able either to put them out of circulation or at least deport them."

Maggie's heart jumped with hope. "Does that mean that we're out of danger?" she asked.

Harry smiled at her affectionately, "Yes, Maggie, I think so. The organization has been squashed with the arrest of these people. Anyone we haven't found probably will run for cover until they're caught. I think the danger to the five of you is past."

Harry leaned forward and continued, "We've watched the house in Hollywood and we've had a tap on the phone since we found it. Last night we got lucky. Two hoodlum types from their organization stumbled out on to Mulholland and flagged down a car. Unfortunately for them, it was one of our unmarked patrol cars. At that point those two didn't seem to mind. They were exhausted and just wanted food and a bed. They were so exhausted that they told all they knew. Then it was easy to pick up Ahmed and the rest of their group. So far Ahmed has refused to talk, but he'll open up. He is a Pakistani, so we may have to deport him. Even so, the threat to you should be over."

Maggie asked, "The two you picked up on Mulholland? What did they look like?"

Harry described The Ferret and Bruno.

Maggie said, "Poor Ferret. Poor Bruno."

Allie said, "Mother, how can you? They wanted to kill us!"

Maggie said, "I know. But somehow, the thought of them climbing that mountain makes me feel sorry for them. They were poor specimens."

Harry looked at Maggie and shook his head. "Don't waste your pity on those two. They aren't worth it!"

Maggie stared at her teacup and frowned. "But, we still don't know exactly what they wanted from us? And what about Hadi?" Turning to Hadi, she asked, "Why did they kidnap you?"

All eyes turned to the mysterious little man. Hadi returned their stares with soft brown eyes and shrugged his shoulders. "Ah, that is a mystery, is it not?"

Harry said, "We'll know more when Ahmed and the others talk. Believe me, sooner or later, they will. He was silent for a moment and then said, "There's one thing more. We think these people have a contact here in the United States. That person or persons will be pretty upset by what's happened. But such a person should be concerned only with lying low or even leaving the country. With this roundup, the backbone of the organization is broken."

Andre turned to Harry and John Landis and asked, "Ah, what do you think was their reason for kidnapping Brigitte and me? What did they want from us? Do you know?"

Harry shook his head, "That's one of the unanswered questions. Because you're the expert in terrorism, they probably thought you'd upset their apple cart. How they thought you'd do that we don't know yet, but I promise you we will." After a thoughtful silence, Harry said, "We'd prefer that you all stay here until every detail has been cleared up. Certainly that's the safest thing. But, if you feel you must go, we're pretty sure it's okay."

Brigitte turned to Andre and murmured a question that Andre answered in French. Then, turning to Harry, Andre said, "We'd like to stay for at least one more day, if we may. Brigitte still is exhausted both physically and emotionally. We need a resting time."

Harry nodded his assent then looked at the others and raised his eyebrows questioningly.

Maggie's eyes met Allie's briefly. Their agreement was instant and silent. To Harry Allie said, "We'll leave soon. It's time we returned to our real lives. But what about the dog? He must belong to someone. What will become of him?"

"Well, I guess we'll call the Humane Society." Then, at Allie's shocked expression, "Or you could take him while we make inquiries. I'll let you know what we find out."

Relief filled Allie's face, "I didn't realize how attached I've become. But I want whatever's best for him." Then, "Oh, I just remembered that my car must still be in front of the condos. I hope it hasn't been towed away."

Harry smiled at her, "We took the liberty of making a spare key and moving it. Actually, it's sitting in the driveway outside right now." The looks on Maggie and Allie's faces at this were reward enough for the hassle he'd had getting the key made and moving the car.

A small silence followed as they assimilated the new turn of events. Their eyes were lowered, almost as if they were afraid to make contact. At last Hadi looked at his fellow refugees and said, "Ah, now, indeed, it is time for us to part." He looked at Maggie fondly, "Yes, dear lady, you were correct. Now that our parting is near, the heart falters, no? It is important for us to remember and to know that we remain family, even when we are apart, yes!"

The others looked at him and at one another, their faces mirroring their feelings of relief, hope, sadness and affection. At last Andre spoke, "It is true. We are family. I feel it. I know it. I will hold each of you in my heart. I will and so will Brigitte. Forever." He bowed his head and blinked his eyes for a moment.

Then, almost without conscious thought or movement, they were on their feet, hugging one another, laughing and crying at the same time.

Maggie found herself facing Hadi. She could not find words to say what she felt, to express her gratitude, to ask the unanswered questions. Hadi stood very still and looked into Maggie's eyes without blinking, his liquid dark eyes filled with love and acceptance. In a quiet sing-song voice he said, "Yes, dear lady. We will meet again. Yes. It is so. Do not distress yourself. Do not concern yourself with the unknowable. It is good, no?"

Maggie gazed back at him through a film of unshed tears and nodded.

Then Hadi turned and walked away, mysterious to the end.

Maggie stood motionless for a long time. Her reverie was interrupted by, "A penny for . . .." She turned to find Harry Cavanaugh at her side.

Maggie smiled shakily and said, "Oh, Harry. How can we thank you for all you've done for us?"

"I only did my job, Maggie. I'm glad it turned out okay. I'm especially glad you and the others are safe. There were some anxious hours when we didn't know where you were or even if . . ." Harry's voice trailed off as he looked down into Maggie's green eyes.

As Maggie returned his look she wondered if Harry could have more than a professional interest in her. But that was just silly. She smiled up at him and said, "Yes, those were anxious times for us. But, you know, they were exciting times, too. It really was quite an adventure." After a pause, "Well, now we go back to our ordinary lives. But, what about you, Harry? What happens next for you? Do you go on to another adventure?"

Harry answered, "Most of the time my work's not very exciting, lots of routine, lots of waiting. You know, not too glamorous." There was a short awkward silence, then Harry continued, "Maggie, when you and Allie. . .er, that is, after you two have rested. . . I mean, I'd like to check in on you or, that is, maybe we could have dinner or something." He finished the last in a rush, and then looked embarrassed.

Maggie smiled broadly and answered, "Why, Harry, that sounds just wonderful. I'd love to have dinner with you. Give me a call and we'll set it up."

"Oh, good. I mean, yes, I will," Harry answered quickly.

Just then Allie walked up and put out her hand to Harry. "Harry, I want to thank you for everything you've done for us.

It was a comfort during our ordeals knowing you were out there somewhere at the other end of the phone. Thank you."

Harry shook her hand vigorously and said, "You're welcome. But it was my job, you know." He glanced quickly at Maggie and looked back to Allie. "I'm glad it turned out okay and you're both safe."

The good-byes continued with hugs, tears, exchanges of addresses and phone numbers. Finally, Maggie and Allie returned to their rooms, followed by Dog, and found their own clothes, freshly laundered and lying on the beds. Quickly, they changed and went back down the stairs.

The white convertible was standing in the bricked drive behind the house. They climbed in and Dog seated himself on Maggie's lap. Maggie scratched behind his ears and laughed. Allie reached behind the seats and handed Maggie her hat. They donned their hats solemnly, looked at each other and broke out laughing. Allie turned the car and with light hearts they started down the drive. Turning, Maggie saw Harry in the doorway. She nudged Allie and they both waved.

Harry waved back, smiling and looking a little forlorn.

"Does he look like an abandoned puppy or what?" Allie asked.

"Yeah, he does sort of, doesn't he? Maggie said nonchalantly.

Allie looked at her mother and raised her eyebrows.

"I don't know, Honey. He did ask me out for dinner. He's a nice man, but I don't know . . ." Maggie's voice trailed off. She shrugged her shoulders in answer to Allie's look.

"Mom! Dinner! All right, Mom! Go for it!" was Allie's irreverent reply.

They giggled and then sighed with contentment. It felt luxurious to be driving, to be free and to feel safe. They wandered down along winding palm lined streets. The sun was warm on their faces and the gusty breezes were warm at their backs.

After a silence, Maggie spoke, "It's hard to believe that it all happened, isn't it?"

"Yes. It is. It'll probably take us a while to integrate it all. Right now, it feels unreal, like a dream," Allie answered.

At the sound of Allie's voice, Dog wiggled and tried to wag his tail. "Allie, what're you going to do about this dog?" Maggie asked.

"Well, Mom, Harry is going to investigate to see if he has an owner somewhere. I think we should do the same. But, he definitely thinks he's my dog. You must admit that!" Allie said laughing.

"There can be no doubt of that," Maggie laughed in return.

"First of all, I suppose he should have a name. Help me think of one. Things've been moving so fast I haven't had a chance to think about him."

The next several minutes were spent brainstorming names. 'Jack' was an obvious and popular suggestion. "He really was like a guardian angel. Did you see how he came barreling down on us when that car was coming in the cemetery?" Maggie asked as she rubbed behind his ears.

"Guardian angel. You're right. Do you think it would be sacrilegious if we called him Gabriel?" Allie glanced at the dog and her mother. Dog's ears pricked up and his little behind wiggled.

"I think Gabriel is perfect." Maggie replied.

"Gabriel." Allie said looking at the dog. "Gabe for short. I think that's it. It fits," she said with a grin. "Okay, Gabe. I guess you've found a new home and a new name!"

Allie turned the car onto a freeway and they headed west toward Malibu and home. As they neared the ocean there was a haze in the air, but Maggie and Allie were so happy to be going home that they barely noticed. The turn off the PCH came up quickly and once again they wound up the switchbacks toward Allie's house. Maggie thought that the neighborhood never had looked so beautiful. Bougainvillea spilled over walls and off porticos, palm tree swayed in the breeze, the sun glinted off their shiny fronds.

Gabe bounced out of the car as soon as it came to a halt in the carport. His demeanor said, 'It's sure good to be home!' Maggie and Allie followed more slowly. Allie's house seemed happy to have them back. Maggie thought the house couldn't be as happy as she was to be here. Wordlessly they wandered upstairs and down, following Gabe's inspection and examining each nook and cranny. "It *feels* okay, clean. I mean, it feels like my house again," Allie said.

Among the messages on the answering machine, Harry Cavanaugh's gruff voice welcoming them home and assuring them that all devices had been removed from the house. Allie and Maggie looked at one another and sighed a silent thank you in unison.

The deck beckoned. Soon they were lounging there with cool drinks staring up through the leafy canopy at the blue sky. In the distance the Pacific glowed, a brilliant blue-green. "Sure is warm today," Allie murmured.

"Sure is. Makes a person want to do nothing, was Maggie's reply.

I need to get to work soon. Phone calls and stuff," Allie said. "But, I seem to have lost my ambition."

"I don't suppose it could be that you are recovering from trauma and exhaustion," Maggie commented.

169

"You're right, Allie said. "That stuff can wait until tomorrow. Let's just lie back and unwind now."

"Suits me." After a long pause, Maggie said, "Allie, what about Max? What was going on with the two of you? Wasn't that an amazing coincidence? Did he remember you from the beach? Are you going to see him again?"

Allie laughed, "Oh, Mom! What about him? I don't know. Yes. No. I don't know!"

Maggie made a face in response.

Allie said, "I really don't know what's going on. He's an attractive man and a most annoying one at times. It was quite a coincidence. And, no. He didn't remember me from the beach, that is, he was remembering *me,* but he couldn't remember where or when. I gave him my number, but who knows when or if he'll do anything with it." Allie sighed ruefully.

Maggie smiled to herself and said, "I'll be surprised if that phone doesn't start ringing very soon. I saw the look in his eyes when he looked at you."

"Well, we'll see, I guess." Allie sat quietly for a while. "Are you hungry? It's well past lunch time."

"Now that you mention it, I'm starved. Let's see what's in the larder." Maggie stretched, climbed out of the chaise, and headed for the kitchen.

Following her Allie said, "I'm not sure what there is. We may have to go out." A soft bark interrupted her. "Oh, my. I just realized I don't have any dog food. We'll have to go out for that at some point. I really should pick up my mail."

Maggie said, "I have a truly decadent idea. Let's hit Brandon's for a snack and run whatever errands are essential. Then let's pick up a movie, French pastries at the bakery and a Thai feast."

"Decadent is right! Chocolate!! Let's do it!"

Gabe was insistent that he go with them. Allie fashioned a makeshift collar and leash from her trunk of horse tack in the carport. Down through the now hazy neighborhood.

Brandon's was bright, cheerful and filled with delicious aromas. Outside Allie tied Gabe to a bicycle rack where he lay down in the shade and sighed. Being in civilization felt strange to Maggie. The meal had a funny sort of *deja vu* quality. She was sure that Allie was feeling it, too. Their last breakfast here seemed long ago, almost as if it had happened in a dream. Would she ever get over this feeling?

"Feels weird, uh?" Allie commented. "Almost as if being here before was a dream, or our adventure was a dream, or now is a dream, or something. It's surreal!"

Maggie thought 'surreal' summed it up nicely.

From Brandon's they walked to the video shop. Choosing a movie took a long time. Finally they settled on two, a romance and a comedy. Adventure films had little appeal.

Gabe stood with his nose into the wind as he and Maggie waited outside while Allie collected her mail. Then, at the market, in addition to dog food and a few things for their kitchen, they purchased a bright red collar and leash. Outside they presented Gabe with his new 'clothes.' He trotted back to the car proudly, showing off his finery.

At the bakery, they bought one of every chocolate pastry offered. On to the Thai restaurant. There they ordered lemon grass coconut soup, curry, noodles, rice, and salad. Up through the neighborhood. A strong wind was tossing the tops of the palm trees. "Mom, d'you think we went a little overboard?"

"Probably. But we're allowed. We deserve it," Maggie answered.

"That's for sure!"

It was nearly dark as they climbed up the switchbacks. The sun was setting in a strange red glow. Maggie wrinkled her nose. "It seems strange that someone would be using their fireplace on such a warm day." Gabe barked his agreement and they laughed.

As they entered the house, they dropped their purses and keys on Maggie's grandmother's sideboard in the hall and went straight to the kitchen where they unloaded their provender. The evening progressed as decadently as they had planned. Satiated on Thai food, they sipped tea and nibbled on the pastries through the first movie. Watching the credits roll down the screen, Maggie stood up, stretched and yawned, "I hate to admit it, but my eyes aren't going to make it through another movie. It's bed for me."

Allie yawned her agreement. Together they stuck the pastries in the refrigerator, tossed empty cartons in the garbage pail and pulled out Maggie's bed.

Maggie lay down, feeling her body relax and melt into the bed. She was asleep almost before Allie made it to the top of the stairs. Allie followed her mother's example. Gabe circled twice, then lay down, nestled at the foot of her bed and peace descended.

Maggie backed down the dark hallway away from something frightening and dreadful at its head. If only she could see what was up there, she could defend herself. But the unknown, whatever it was, was so evil, so terrifying, that she could not approach it and it remained a mystery. Slowly she inched backward, unable to run, unable to turn her back on the fearful something. As she backed down the hall she heard a whispering voice, "Dear lady, dear lady, please be careful. Please be careful. You must leave. You must leave now."

Hadi! It was Hadi. But where? Where is he? Maggie looked around. Nothing. All was in darkness. She called out, "Hadi? Hadi? Where are you?"

Maggie flopped over in bed and sat bolt upright, her eyes squeezed shut. It was too scary to open them. She shuddered as she realized that she had been dreaming. Slowly she opened her eyes. Darkness. The lighter rectangle of the window above her showed a wild night, with trees bending in the wind. Maggie sighed and leaned back against the pillows. Her breathing quieted.

A dream. But what a dream! Ugh! Only the young had the constitution to combine curry and chocolate late at night! Whatever possessed her to eat so recklessly? Maggie thought about Hadi, trying to shake off the feeling of the dream. But the sense of danger persisted.

She lay down again and closed her eyes. They wouldn't stay closed. She lay in bed staring at the ceiling, listening to the sounds of the night. The wind howled around the house whistling through any little crack it could find. The screen door rattled on its hinges. A tree branch banged against the deck. Between blasts of wind, Maggie could hear a gentle wheeze from upstairs. Gabe was snoring.

Even though it had been just a dream, Maggie was left with a sense of impending doom that she couldn't shake. Hadi's warning had seemed especially real. Her thoughts focused on Hadi. Who was he really? Where was he now? Hadi never had mentioned a home or even what country he was from. She realized that she knew almost nothing about Hadi's life in those respects and yet she felt that in another way she knew him very well. Strange.

Her thoughts were interrupted by the sound of toenails coming down the stairs. A small damp nose nuzzled her hand.

Maggie scratched behind Gabe's ears.   He circled twice, lay down next to her and sighed.

Chapter Fourteen

"Grrrrr!! Grrrr!!" Maggie was awakened by low menacing growls from Gabe. She put her hand down and found the hair on his back bristled. At her touch there was a small welcoming wag of his tail. But the growling continued.

"What is it?" she whispered. Outside the wind seemed stronger and noisier. She could hear nothing except the howl of the wind and accompanying sounds. The screen door was banging even more violently now and the pounding on the deck had become a steady tattoo.

Suddenly she heard a particularly strong gust of wind and a crash. The potted palm on the deck must have blown over. Maggie jumped up out of bed and rushed toward the door to the deck, intent on rescuing the plant. Not wanting to awaken Allie, Maggie chose not to turn on a light. Through the sliding glass door she could see the overturned palm rolling from side to side in the wind. Impulsively, she opened the door and stepped outside. The wind caught at her nightgown and it became a sail billowing out around her. Maggie nearly was knocked off her feet. On all fours she crawled to the pot end of the palm and tugged. Grunting, she heaved on the pot, a few inches, then a few more. Maggie closed her eyes, set her bare feet on the wood of the deck floor and pulled again. She rolled the pot a little and pulled. Roll and pull. Roll and pull. Maggie kept her eyes closed because the air was filled with dust and leaves and twigs. Slowly, slowly, she pulled the battered plant toward the door. Then over the threshold, finally into the house. One more tug. Maggie sat back on her heels and toppled over backward, grateful to be in the comparative shelter of the house. She lay back, panting, waiting to catch her breath. Beside her Gabe jumped up and down, barking sharp little barks of encouragement. "Shhh." she gasped. "Shhh."

"What's up, Mom?" came a sleepy voice from the stairs. The lights came on and then as Allie saw her mother prostrate on the floor, her voice rose in alarm, "Mom, are you okay? What's happening?"

Maggie rolled over and grinned, "Your silly mother is having adventures in the night! This plant's screams of distress woke me and I had to rescue it!" Maggie panted and laughed at the same time.

Allie sighed with relief, "Oh, thank God! I was afraid something awful had happened. What a night! I don't remember the wind ever being so intense. Here, let me get that plant inside so we can close the door." Together Allie and Maggie pulled the plant the rest of the way into the room and set it upright while Gabe danced around them barking.

"Wow! What time is it?"

"Around three, I think." Gabe's barking reached a crescendo. "Shhh, Gabe. You'll wake the neighborhood," Maggie said.

"Thanks for saving the palm. As wild as that wind is, I'm afraid it would have been a goner by morning," Allie said groggily. "Are you still sleepy? Let's see if we can get back to sleep." She turned and started up the stairs.

Maggie turned to say goodnight for the second time when a deep voice behind them said, "Miss McGill, I think it would be better if you stayed up a little longer."

"What. . .?"

"Who. . .?"

Allie and Maggie twirled around as one person, their eyes wide, their faces white.

Maggie's heart pounded as she recognized the large white-haired man holding a small, business-like gun, his arm stretched out unnaturally in front of him. Allie recovered her voice first. "Dr. Albright. What are you doing here?"

Maggie recognized Dr. John Albright from the San Francisco party. She remembered how her skin had crawled during their brief conversation. She remembered her instant and unreasonable dislike of the man, despite his distinguished appearance and seeming affability. He did not look distinguished now and he definitely was not being affable. His mane of white hair was standing on end from the wind. His khaki slacks and windbreaker were rumpled, dusty and covered with bits of debris. His chin was grizzled with a day's growth of beard. Even more disturbing was the look in his china blue eyes. It was as if a veneer of socially accepted behavior, a facade of civilization had been removed. His eyes had a wild and raw look that was primal, the look of a crazed predator.

Maggie glanced at Allie, then back to John Albright. It seemed she could hear Hadi's voice telling her to breath deeply and stay calm. She took a deep breath and said quietly, "Dr.

Albright, I am surprised to see you. Won't you come in and sit down." She reached behind her and pulled on her bathrobe.

The normalcy of her greeting and the invitation seemed to throw their visitor off guard. He took a few steps toward a chair, then stopped and said, "You two! What are you trying to do? It won't work, you know. I know about you."

Maggie continued as if he had not spoken, "Oh, Dr. Albright. You've caught us unprepared. Here. Let me just fold up this bed and make a comfortable place for you to sit." So saying, she then bent down and hurriedly stripped off the bed linens and with Allie's help folded up the sofa.

John Albright stared at the two women, his mouth slightly agape, as if he could not take in what they were saying and doing.

Allie, sensing her mother's strategy, said, "Please do have a seat, Dr. Albright. Can I get you a cup of tea?" She walked into the kitchen and turned the gas on under the shiny tea kettle.

"Here. Wait a minute. What are you trying to do?" Albright stammered. "You, young woman. You come right back in here. Of course, I don't want any tea. I've come to have it out with the two of you and to take care of you."

Maggie did not like the sound of that. Her skin was crawling and the little hairs on the back of her neck were standing up. She looked into those dreadful blue eyes, smiled and said, "Well, Dr. Albright, if you have something to discuss with us, we may as well be comfortable while we do it. Won't you just have a seat. We'd be happy to make you a cup of tea or give you a glass of juice if you like, but, if not, let's just sit down and discuss the matter calmly."

Allie leaned against the bar that separated the kitchen from the living room and smiled, also. "So, Dr. Albright. What's on your mind?" To herself, she wondered how much mind was left for him to have anything on!

Albright looked from one of them to the other uncertainly, then gingerly sat on the edge of Allie's only easy chair. An awkward silence ensued. Maggie was not sure how to proceed. One thing was certain. Of all their adventures, this was the very most dangerous. Clearly Dr. Albright was not well mentally and therefore not in any way predictable. Maggie wished she had more experience treating the seriously mentally ill.

In the silence, the telephone rang. The three of them jumped as one and Albright waved the gun at the two women. "Don't answer it. Let it ring."

They listened. One, two, three rings. On the fourth, the answering machine responded. Then as they listened, a tired, frightened voice said, "Allie! Maggie! Harry Cavanaugh here. Are you there? If so, please pick up. I know it's an unreasonable hour, but this is important. Maybe you already know and you've left. I hope so. There are fires. The whole Malibu area is burning. There are fires in Malibu and Topanga canyons. Several homes have burned already. If it comes up that canyon behind you with this wind, you might not have time to get away. I'd advise you leave right now and try a hotel in Santa Monica or the Marina. Call me when you get this message and let me know where you are. Well, anyway, I hope you've already gone. Bye." The voice trailed off and he hung up.

Maggie and Allie looked at one another then at John Albright. He appeared not to have heard the message. Maggie said, "Dr. Albright, it seems there are wild fires in the canyons tonight. It could be dangerous for all of us. Could we drive down to a restaurant and have something to eat and talk over whatever is bothering you?"

John Albright looked at them from glazed eyes and said disdainfully, "You two are so clever! You think you can fool me. Well, you've met your match with me. I'll not be tricked by phony telephone messages. Who is Harry Cavanaugh, anyway? Who does he think he is to interrupt when we have important business to discuss?"

Allie said from the kitchen bar, "Oh, Harry's just an old friend of the family. He's retired. He sort of takes care of us."

"Retired. I'm going to retire. I didn't want to retire so soon. But now I have to leave and retire," Albright mumbled. He pulled his head up and fixed his blue eyes on first Allie and then Maggie and said, "But you! You've tried to spoil my plans. You were going to tell everyone. No one must know. It must stay a secret. You two would tell the whole world."

Maggie glanced at Allie, trying to make sense of this last. Just then the teakettle whistled behind Allie. She turned to extinguish the gas, but John Albright stood up and waved the gun. "Where are you going? What's that noise?"

Allie stopped and stood very still. Above the shrill of the tea kettle she said, "It's okay, Dr. Albright. The teakettle is hot. I was just going to turn it off." Slowly, she moved into the kitchen, keeping her eyes on the gun. Slowly, slowly, she reached down and turned the gas off. The shrill whistling stopped and Maggie breathed a sigh of relief.

"You come back in here, young lady, and sit down this minute." Albright sounded like an enraged parent. Allie moved back into the living room and took a seat beside her mother.

Allie looked John Albright in the eyes and said, "Well, Dr. Albright. Maybe you'd like to tell us what's troubling you. I can assure you that neither my mother nor I wish you any harm. There must be some misunderstanding. Let's see if we can clear it up."

Albright's eyes glared at them. "Clear it up? Clear it up! There's nothing you can do to clear it up. It's too late now. Much too late. It's all your fault. If you'd just kept out of it. If only you hadn't meddled. . .but you did. And now, it's all gone. Everything destroyed. All your fault. . ." his voice trailed off peevishly.

Maggie leaned forward and said, "Do I understand you to say that you think Allie and I have interfered in your affairs and created a problem?"

Albright stormed, "Created a problem! You haven't 'created a problem'! You've ruined everything! Don't talk to me about creating a problem!"

Soothingly Maggie said, "Forgive me. It was an unfortunate choice of words. But Allie and I are trying to understand what's distressing you so."

Albright answered, his voice now a low menacing monotone, "What's distressing me so? What's distressing me! Let me tell you what's distressing me. It was all arranged. I've worked long and hard and it all was arranged. The plans were made. Everything was going like clockwork. No problems. No hitches. Like clockwork. Ahmed was doing his part over there. I was doing mine here. Our organization was working perfectly. We were winning. It only needed one final thing. One event. And that would show everyone. The world would know. It would be a consummate victory. And I. I'd lead this country into a higher vision. I'd save this country for Allah. But now! Now there's nothing left for me but exile and retirement. *That* is what is distressing me. And it's your fault! You did it!"

At the mention of Ahmed's name Maggie and Allie looked at one another. It wasn't over yet. Harry had made a mistake. There was this one last loose end.

Allie said, "Tell us about your organization, Dr. Albright. What was its purpose?"

John Albright looked at her in surprise, "How do you know about the organization? Well, no matter now. We were working to free the world of the scourge of the materialism of the infidel. Ahmed worked in his country and I. . .I had the most important part. Here in this country I was the leader. Here I created a strong organization that was completely secret. No one even guessed its existence. We had many victories, large and small, and we were planning the most ambitious one of all, the final victory. After that, the unrest created would topple this government and we could take over. It was perfect. We'd secure this country for the one true God." As he talked, Albright's eyes became brighter and the glazed look lifted.

Outside, the wind continued to rage and it carried an ever increasingly strong odor of smoke. Maggie spoke again soothingly, "It sounds as if you worked very hard for your beliefs, Dr. Albright. It can be upsetting when one's plans don't work out. Why don't we three drive down to the highway where we could find something to eat and you can tell us more."

"Do you women ever think about anything but food!" Albright stormed again. "I'll leave after awhile, but you'll not go with me!"

Again Maggie could hear Hadi inside her head telling her to remain calm, to breath deeply, to send soothing energy into the room. "Yes, that is fine with us, Dr. Albright. Won't you tell us exactly what your plans were. You know, we really would be interested. We know so little."

Albright's back stiffened. He threw his head up and tossed the trailing white hair out of his eyes. "The plans were secret, but no matter now. You'll never tell anyone. Why not? I may as well tell you. Yes. All right. The ultimate mission of our organization, of course, is to bring Islam to the whole world. It is the only true faith. We've been besieged by infidels. But, no matter. We've had our successes. The bombing of the Hotel St. Mary. Do you remember that? How many were killed?"

Maggie and Allie exchanged glances, then nodded encouragingly to Albright.

He continued, "That was perfectly planned and executed. A perfect mission. They still don't have a clue about who was behind it. After that, the police commissioner lost his job and was replaced by someone who looks the other way. The mayor was not reelected. So much fear was created that the residents of that city were ready to accept any form of government that would provide safety. There've been other incidents, other victories, but I won't tell you about them now."

Allie asked softly, "But what about us? How is it that we've become involved?"

At that Albright's face suffused with blood and his eyes became even wilder. "How? You dare to ask me how! You! You!. . ." He sputtered. Then, making an obvious effort to control himself, he said in a quieter voice, "It was perfectly planned and it was going perfectly. The trouble started was when Charles Sandoval and Ed Martin wanted to hire Andre Fouchet for the spring semester. The fools! Fouchet is a very dangerous man. He's the one person who might have noticed the connections between FLO and our organization. It was imperative to discourage his taking the position. But even that would not have stopped us. We'd have found a way to stop him."

John Albright stopped and looked at Maggie and Allie, almost as if he were asking for their approval.

Maggie sat quietly, afraid to say anything that might anger him further. Allie didn't move a muscle.

Soon John Albright continued. "Yes, we could've dealt with Andre Fouchet, but then the two of you interfered. It was too much. We tried to discourage you. Any normal person would've quit after a rock fell on them in the park, but not you! Just who are you working for anyway?"

He didn't give them an opportunity to respond, but looked at Maggie and went on. "Ahmed saw you talking to the Fouchets on the plane. Then, when the two of you left the airport, you took a photograph of me in the limousine with Baha Aflaki, our spiritual leader here and my assistant. If Andre Fouchet had seen that photo, it would've been the end of everything. It was imperative that no one knows of my connection to our organization. Oh, you thought you were very clever, pretending to be tourists! So innocent! I need that photograph. Where is it? Now that Ahmed and Baha and the others have been arrested, they'll be looking for any other members of our organization. No one knows about me. Ahmed and Baha won't talk. But that photograph could ruin everything. Where is it? I must have it!" John Albright stopped talking and glared at Maggie and Allie.

There was a silence. Finally Maggie answered, glancing first at Allie and then looking at Albright, "I don't have it. But, at least now, I know what you're talking about. Of course, I would've given it to you or to Ahmed from the beginning if I'd known what you wanted. Oh, now it all makes sense!"

"You don't have it!" thundered Albright. He jumped to his feet and waved the gun. "How can you sit there and tell me you don't have it? I don't believe you!"

"But it's true, really, it is. The photo you are asking about must be the one I snapped of Allie outside the airport. I sort of remember that there was a limo in the background. But, truly, Dr. Albright, I didn't see you in it. I've not seen the photo. It hasn't been developed yet." As she spoke Maggie remembered that she left that particular roll of film at the drug store in Malibu before their abduction. Should she tell Albright that? Her first concern was getting Allie and herself out of this dangerous situation. She feared he might carry out his threat if he knew where to find the photo. So she said, "I'm not sure where that roll of film is. I removed it from the camera and intended to take it to be developed, but then we were kidnapped. I'm not sure where it is right now. But we'll find it tomorrow and you may have it when we do."

Silence followed this last statement. Albright looked at the two women with glazed eyes, almost as if he could not comprehend what had been said. The wind was throwing small objects against the windows, the doors rattled on their hinges. The smell of smoke was stronger than ever. Gabe lay quietly under the coffee table where he had retreated when John Albright entered the room. The hair standing up on his back was the only indication that he was not asleep.

The telephone rang once again breaking the uneasy silence. Albright's head jerked up and his cold blue eyes focused on the two women. They listened for the message. "Hello? Uh, this is Max LaCroix. Miss McGill? er Allie? I just wanted to call to see if you're there. I guess you're not. Well, that's good. Er, that is, I'm sorry to miss you, but I called to warn you about the fires. I'm not sure just where you live, but the Malibu hills are burning. Maybe you haven't returned yet from the safe house, or maybe you have and now you have gone to a hotel or something. Well, anyway, I'm glad you're not in danger! Er, good-bye. Let's talk soon." The deep voice stopped, cleared its throat and hung up.

Allie stood up and said, "Dr. Albright, I fear we may be in some danger here from the fire. The smell of smoke is getting stronger. Let's just drive down to the highway and find a nice quiet place where we can talk this out." She moved ever so slowly as she talked, inching her way around the coffee table, toward John Albright.

Maggie watched Allie's progress without looking at her and wondered what she was planning. Slowly, slowly, an inch at a time, Allie moved around the bleached oak coffee table, her bare feet sliding through the furry nap of the thick white rug.

The professor stared at Allie's face without speaking, as if he were trying to translate a foreign language. He seemed unaware of her movement toward him.

Maggie wondered if he was able to understand the danger the fire presented to all of them. Her experience with the seriously mentally ill was limited, but she realized that Dr. Albright might be so disoriented that a wild fire would not seem threatening to him. It seemed to her that she was watching him move from one reality to another in fairly rapid shifts. It also seemed that his moments of lucidity were becoming fewer and shorter as time went on.

Maggie spoke softly, as if she were speaking to a frightened animal, "Dr. Albright, it is going to be all right. There's nothing for us to worry about. Let's just relax. Everything will be okay. Soon we can go down the hill away from the danger of this fire. Then we can talk this out. I'm sure that we'll find the photo in the morning. There really is nothing for us to fear. . .." Quietly, slowly she talked, almost crooned, to the nervous man, never taking her eyes from Albright's face. As Maggie spoke, Allie continued to inch her way around the coffee table. Albright shifted his stare to Maggie, as if mesmerized by the sound of her voice.

Outside, the wind was as wild as ever. Smoke filled the living room now and stung their eyes. Through the windows the sky had taken on a dark red glow. The air inside the guesthouse was warm and close.

Maggie found it increasingly difficult to look into Albright's eyes. They were wild and vacant. Her heart beat faster when she noticed the red glow from the corner of her eye. But she did not dare to break eye contact with Albright. She was not sure what Allie planned, but clearly she was intent on moving around the coffee table. So Maggie continued her soft crooning talk, animal talk, talk to quiet a wild heart, talk for the caged tiger, talk for the trapped beast. John Albright stood immobile, staring at Maggie, his jaw slack, but his grasp on the gun never wavering.

Allie reached the breakfast bar and inched around it. Through the large glass doors behind Albright, flickering lights could be seen. Could the fire be so close? How long could they remain here and still escape? It seemed unbelievably true that the fire was coming this way.

Maggie's peripheral vision showed Allie in the kitchen near the stove.

The flickering light became more pronounced. There was more light outside. Suddenly, with a great whoosh sound, the tall eucalyptus outside was in flames. The bright firelight filled the living room. They could feel the heat through the glass.

Albright's head jerked up and he glanced over his shoulder at the blazing tree. Across the street, flames could be seen on the roof of the Asherman's house. It was as if the fire had brought Albright back from a distant land. He shouted at Allie, "What are you doing in there? Get back out here this minute!" Albright pointed the gun directly at Allie. Maggie could see his finger begin to squeeze the trigger. Her heart stopped beating.

At that moment Gabe leapt out from under the coffee table, his small hard body a projectile aimed at Albright's extended arm. The gun went off. The shot was wild and the bullet landed in the beam above Allie's head. Caught off guard, Albright twirled to ward off his furry attacker. Maggie jumped onto the coffee table, intent on grabbing the gun. He fired again. A vase on the shelf behind Maggie shattered. She reached for the gun, but missed as Albright brought his arm down, aiming at Gabe who was dancing in circles around his feet, planting fierce nips in his target's ankles. In the kitchen Allie grabbed the teakettle and flung the scalding water across the breakfast bar at Albright's head. Albright was twirling in an attempt to keep up with his three adversaries. The nearly boiling water caught him in the face. Maggie would remember the scream for a long time.

Allie grabbed Maggie's hand and pulled her from the coffee table. Holding hands they raced for the door. Allie scraped the keys from the sideboard as they shot out of the door into a violent, foreign world. Angry red light, choking smoke, small fiery missiles filled the air, it was snowing fire! The heat was intense. It was like running into a huge oven. They ran down the flagged walk. Gabe ran ahead but without barking. Flames filled the trees. Over their heads the house was blazing. Just as they reached the steps leading to the carport, they heard a gunshot behind them. Albright! He was coming out of the door, firing at them. He was terrible to see, wild, insanely wild. He fired the gun again. There was a soft thud sound in the wooden railing by Maggie's right shoulder. A bullet! It could have hit either one of them! Up the steps. Up. Maggie's legs felt leaden. Her breath was coming in gasps. Allie pulled at her arm. Maggie looked over her shoulder. The huge eucalyptus was a flaming tower. Albright ran down the walk toward them. Could they get away in time? Then, just as they reached the top of the steps, with a deafening crash, the eucalyptus fell across the house, across the flagged walk, across Allie's geraniums, across John Albright. This time there was no scream. He made no sound at all. The vegetation along the walk burst into flames. Albright's body was enveloped in flames. The fire raced toward the two women.

"Allie," Maggie gasped.

"I know," Allie said. "Come on. There's nothing we can do. Let's go! Come on! Come!" Allie pulled Maggie to the car. The carport was not yet burning. But the house was in flames. It seemed as if the fire was everywhere. Allie turned on the hose tap and sprayed the top of the convertible. Then she soaked two towels she kept there for washing her car. "Here, Mom. Put this over your nose and mouth." So saying, she tied a wet towel across her face bandit style. As they got into the car Gabe jumped in also and situated himself on Maggie's lap. Maggie shared a corner of her wet towel with him.

"Hold on! We're getting out of here!" Allie shot the little car out of the carport, shifted gears and they started down the hill. Maggie thought she would never forget that ride. The little car raced through walls of flame on either side of the street for the first few blocks. The air was filled with fire snow; large fluffy bits of red ash filled the air. The heat was intense. The heat and the smoke made breathing painful. When they reached the lower levels of the neighborhood the fires were scattered, with a house here and there still not burning. On the lowest levels only an occasional house was aflame.

The Pacific Coast Highway was filled with fire trucks and emergency vehicles. Red and blue flashing lights filled the night. They were flagged down by a tired looking policeman. He leaned in the window and said sternly, "You shouldn't be here. How'd you get in here? Where'd you come from?"

Allie's voice was a faint croak, "We just came from my house up there." She pointed up at the flaming hillside.

"You did? Here. Follow me." He mounted a motorcycle parked beside the road and started down the highway.

"What do you suppose he intends to do to us?" Maggie whispered. She was surprised to find that her voice was almost gone. Only then did she realize that tears were streaming down her face. She glanced at the next seat and found Allie's face also wet with tears.

"I don't know and I don't much care so long as he doesn't send us back up there," Allie croaked grimly.

The motorcycle stopped beside an ambulance-like trailer. Walking back to the convertible, the policeman said, "Let's get you in here. You may need to go to the hospital for treatment." He opened the car door and motioned them out. Maggie and Allie got out of the car and walked beside the policeman to the open back door of the medical trailer. Maggie continued to hold Gabe tightly to her chest.

The emergency medical team was solicitous and efficient. Soon both Maggie and Allie were receiving oxygen. With burning eyes Maggie looked around. Little Gabe was uncharacteristically quiet on Allie's lap.

One of the doctors saw her look. Gently he picked up the little dog and examined him. Then without a word he fitted an oxygen mask over the dog's nose. He improvised with plastic wrap and tape so that it fit snugly. Gabe sat quietly, permitting these ministrations as if he understood what was happening. Allie motioned her thanks.

The medical team chatted softly as they worked, lifting the spirits of their patients. The other patients were fire fighters who were receiving treatment similar to that given to Allie and Maggie.

Maggie could feel her strength returning with the oxygen therapy. She could see color returning to Allie's pale face. Even Gabe looked perkier. Eventually they were released with an admonition to consult their private physician tomorrow and to seek emergency treatment if their coughs continued more than a day or if they experienced any breathing difficulties.

The sun was rising as they headed south along a bizarrely different PCH. The only traffic was emergency vehicles. Neither of them looked up at the hillside or behind them as Allie drove sedately through the barricades into a more normal seeming world.

Allie turned onto Sunset Boulevard and then onto a side street and stopped. She turned to her mother with tears in her eyes. "Mom, I don't know where to go. We don't have a home anymore." A sob caught in her throat. The tears spilled over and ran down her cheeks.

Maggie's eyes filled with tears as she looked into her daughter's face. "I know. We're been through a lot. That place is gone. And your beautiful things are gone, too. But, Honey, we are our home. We can find another place. We are alive and we have each other. It will be okay. Do you want me to drive?"

"Yeah, would you? Please."

Solemnly they traded seats. Gabe watched with big eyes. Then he climbed into Allie's lap and licked her face in an effort to console her. Allie looked at Maggie and grinned; then she burst into tears again.

Maggie reached out and put her arms around Allie. "Go ahead, Sweetie, cry it out. Tears streamed down Maggie's face as she held her sobbing daughter. She was crying in sympathy for Allie's feelings; she was crying for her own loss and for the loss of the beautiful place; she was crying in release of the stress, fatigue and pain of the last few days.

Finally, Maggie's eyes dried. She straightened and retrieved her arm. Then she sat still for a moment, gathering her wits, trying to think about the next move. A bed and a hot shower would be nice. Only then did she realize that both of them were still in their nightclothes. Thank goodness, she thought, that she had covered her thin gown with a robe when John Albright had surprised them. Allie's white cotton pajamas were stained with soot but, at least, they were not transparent. Where could they present themselves with no clothes, no money, no credit cards, in fact, with nothing at all? Then she remembered Harry Cavanaugh. Maggie started the car and turned back down to the PCH.

When she explained her plight to the service station attendant she was given the use of the telephone and offered coffee and donuts. She punched in Harry's number. A sleepy, "Yes?"

"Harry, this is. . ."

"Hello, Maggie," Harry interrupted. "Where are you? Are you all right? I tried to call you."

"Yes, yes, I know," Maggie answered. "Well, the truth is, Harry, we're in a sort of a fix." Maggie gave Harry the significant high points of their most recent adventure. "Harry, the thing is, we are at this gas station on the PCH and we don't have any money or purses or anything. And we're still in our nightclothes. I'm not sure what to do next. Then I remembered your number. . .." Her voice trailed off.

"Oh, Maggie. Are the two of you okay? I mean, physically. Were you hurt? Did you have smoke inhalation?"

Maggie told him the details of their medical treatment.

"Well, I think you need a quiet bed and a hot shower to begin with," Harry said.

At the mention of the shower Maggie nodded her head. Allie watching from the car wondered who her mother was talking to for so long.

"That sounds like heaven right now," Maggie said.

"Where exactly are you?" Harry asked. When she had told him, Harry directed her to an early morning coffee shop where he promised to meet her.

Harry was in the parking lot as promised driving a large silver sedan. He had brought a companion who Maggie recognized from the last time Harry had rescued them. "Pete can follow us in your car if you'd like to ride with me," Harry said. Gratefully Maggie and Allie crawled into the wide back seat of the silver car. Maggie surrendered the convertible's keys to a smiling Pete. Gabe snuggled on the seat between the two women.

Chapter Fifteen

Walking through the streets of San Francisco at dusk. The air was cool and moist. A delicious aroma drifted out of a door. Mmmm! Garlic. Caesar salad? Pasta? Crusty bread? Maggie realized she was hungry, not only hungry, ravenous. She twirled around to enter the door. . ..

Maggie woke as her body twisted off the bed. She crawled back on the bed and lay still for a moment trying to figure out where she was. Then the memories came back in a flood. The fire. John Albright. Harry. Maggie smiled when she thought about Harry. He had brought them to the safe house. Maggie had only vague memories of their arrival here, of climbing the stairs to their old rooms, of falling into bed. Across the room she saw Allie still sleeping peacefully. Gabe, curled up at the foot of her bed, was snoring softly.

A pang in her stomach brought the dream back. Hungry! Maggie thought she never had felt so hungry. The aromas drifting up from the kitchen were intoxicating. Whatever were they cooking? What time is it. She looked at the bedside clock.

Eight. Eight o'clock! That must be dinner I am smelling she thought? Maggie's feet hit the floor and she headed for the bathroom. The mirror showed a disheveled person with black smudges on her face, hair standing on end. Ugh! Her nightgown had a rip on the shoulder.

She found new toothbrushes and toilet articles in a basket on the bathroom counter. While she was brushing her teeth Allie appeared at the door. "Hi, Mom. What's up?"

"I am. I'm starving. I plan to make myself just presentable and get downstairs as quickly as possible."

Allie wrinkled her nose. "Ummm. Smells good. What time is it?"

In response Maggie pointed to the clock.

"I can't believe it. Wow."

They bathed and dressed as quickly as possible. Once again they found clothing laid out on the chairs. In the dining room they found Harry and Fritz lingering over dessert and coffee. As they entered the two men stood up and Harry walked around the table to greet them. "Hello, how're you two feeling this evening? Did you rest well? Are you hungry?"

"Yes!" Maggie and Allie answered in unison.

"We are famished," Allie said.

As she spoke, Mildred entered with a tray of food. Silence ensued as the two hungry women dealt with the food. Maggie smiled her no thanks when Mildred offered seconds. Just as Maggie was leaning back in her chair John Landis entered the dining room. He greeted them warmly, then asked if they felt up to talking about their latest adventure.

"Well, yes, I think it might be a good idea. The sooner we talk about it, the sooner we can begin to let go of it. It was pretty intense, you know," Maggie answered.

Harry raised his eyebrows in a questioning way to John Landis.

"Maggie, Allie, I wonder if you'd object to having the Fouchets sit in on this interview? They're still here, you know," Landis said. "They might help us fill in the pieces of this puzzle."

"Andre? Brigitte? Where? We'd love to see them. Yes, please. Do invite them," Allie answered as Maggie nodded her head in agreement.

"Harry? What about Hadi? Is he here still?" Maggie asked.

Harry shook his head. "We don't know where he is. He left soon after you two did and we haven't heard from him since."

They sipped tea while Mildred went upstairs and returned with Andre and Brigitte. For Maggie, seeing the honeymooners felt like being reunited with family. The greetings were warm, with exclamations and questions in a sort of French/English mélange that had developed during their trip across the mountains. Andre and Brigitte both looked rested and relaxed. Maggie remembered vividly their first meeting on the airplane.

Harry said, "We invited a guy from Foreign Learning Opportunities to be here. He's flying down from San Francisco. I expected him to be here by now. I want him to hear your story, but let's not wait any longer. Let's hear what happened to you two last night."

Maggie started to tell them about the wind and the fallen palm on the deck when Ed rushed in, a little out of breath. Introductions and greetings were exchanged. Ed held Allie's hand for just a moment longer than necessary and said, "I'm so glad to see you alive and well. I understand you have had several narrow escapes. Please tell us about them."

Allie and Maggie told their story together, one filling in what the other forgot. They talked with only an occasional question for clarification for over an hour. As they described their fear, Albright's gun and the fire, Harry's face became even more grave. At last, as their story came to an end, they stopped.

Maggie broke the silence, "I understand so much more now about all our adventures. But, you know, one thing still puzzles me. What was their goal here in the United States? What was their next big project? Dr. Albright never told us. And we were so intent on escaping that we didn't even think to ask him." Maggie's brow was furrowed with puzzlement.

"Oh, I can tell you that," Harry answered. "Aside from just hating us for being Americans. They wanted to create panic and chaos that would disrupt stability of the government and perhaps eventually cause it to fail. Then they could move in and take over."

"But he told us that," interrupted Allie. "What he didn't tell us was what their next target was. I had the impression that they had something big planned."

Harry and John exchanged glances. "Our questioning of the other people we picked up has given us some insight on their plans. What we had not yet discovered was Albright's identity. It is interesting how they continued to protect him even when it was clear that it was all over," John said.

Harry continued, "One of the reasons we wanted both Andre and Ed here is that we think FLO was their target. Turning to Andre and Ed he asked, "Do you have any ideas about when and where they planned to do that?"

As Harry was speaking, Ed became agitated, shifting his weight in his chair and breathing more rapidly. When he answered his voice was tight with excitement, "Yes. I think I might. You see, because of the travel expenses, our programs tend to draw mostly well-to-do students. It is true that we have some scholarships, but mostly we draw students from affluent families. We also have very high scholastic standards. So our students tend to be a specialized population—both highly intelligent and representing families of the leaders of our society.

Andre added, "That is just the population that a terrorist organization would like to hit."

Ed continued, "However, because our students go to many different areas around the world, normally they never meet together and so it would have been difficult to attack this population as a group. But this year is different. This year we have a three-day orientation seminar scheduled for the second week in January in the Bay area. All our students are required to attend. They leave from the seminar for their various destinations around the world. We have over eight hundred students enrolled this year."

Now Andre was the excited one. "Eight hundred of the brightest and most economically advantaged young people! What an enticing target for a terrorist! It would be hitting capitalism and the whole system where it would hurt most. A bomb placed at one of the meetings would have given them just the type of attention they want. This must be what they had planned. It must be!"

Harry said, "Good. Those guys will open up now that we know what to ask and especially now that Albright's gone. They won't have a reason to protect him."

Maggie shuddered, "But what a horrible thing! How could that man have done that? He was an educator. He had worked with these youngsters for years. How could he have sanctioned. . . no, *planned*. How could he have planned such a horrible thing?"

Allie squeezed her mother's hand, "Mom, you saw him. You saw his eyes. He was gone. Somehow, he was gone. We don't know what happened to him, but sometime, somehow, something must have snapped. That man in our house wasn't the same one who has worked with this program for so many years."

Ed said, "That must be so. I knew him and worked with him for over eight years. In the beginning he seemed inspired, completely dedicated to the program. But in later years it was as if he let up a little. I thought it simply was that he was getting older and was tired. But apparently there was more to it than that."

Thoughtfully Maggie said, "So now we know why they kidnapped Allie and me. And we know what they wanted from Andre and Brigitte. But what about Hadi? Do you know why they kidnapped Hadi?"

Harry glanced at John Landis and said, "Hadi is a very mysterious character. He wouldn't give us any information about why they were holding him. And he didn't tell us anything about himself. Clearly they must've seen him as a threat. Even now, they refuse to talk about him. When he left here he disappeared. We don't know even if he still is in the country. Very mysterious."

Maggie sighed. After a silence she said, "You know, it strikes me as interesting that Hadi paid homage to Allah. So his religion would be Islam, no?"

She raised her eyebrows and looked around the table. She was greeted by nods.

"Well, the religion of Ahmed and Dr. Albright also is Islam. Isn't it interesting that two different groups can observe the same religion and come up with diametrically opposed conclusions?" Again, nods and silence. "But, then, perhaps one shouldn't be so surprised. It really is what man does with a belief rather than the belief itself that creates either good or evil. I mean, look at Christianity. We have many different believers that call themselves Christian. Some really bizarre things have been done in the name of Christianity. I mean, look at the Inquisition, for example. I suppose man is capable of twisting anything to fit his own purposes, or perhaps, his own sickness. No?"

Allie smiled at her mother, "Don't you think, Mom, that how one interprets a belief system has more to do with what is inside that person than with the belief system itself?"

Their eyes met over the table and Maggie gave her daughter a loving nod, "As with almost everything. Look at the many different interpretations we have of the United States Constitution."

The group pondered this for a while. And then the conversation continued until the small hours of the morning. Maggie found it increasingly difficult to hold her eyes open. Harry caught her nodding and gave her a sweet conspiratorial smile. "I see that our guests of honor still are feeling the effects of their ordeal. Shall we call it a night?"

As if in a dream, Maggie said goodnight to the others. She noticed Allie and Ed talking together in low voices, but she was too sleepy even to feel curious. Upstairs she was asleep as soon as her head hit the pillow.

The next morning Maggie and Allie lingered over breakfast discussing their options and the mechanics of putting their lives back together. Maggie spent some time on the telephone rearranging her travel plans so that she could remain in California for extra time to help Allie with what seemed the nearly impossible task of starting again.

Harry Cavanaugh offered them lodging at the safe house until they could find another place for Allie to live. He was helpful in arranging for the replacement of their drivers' licenses and credit cards. Television and radio reported the full scope of the fire disaster. A short announcement stated that Dr. John Albright, noted educator, was one of the fire casualties. No mention was made of the other circumstances of his death.

Maggie and Allie took Gabe to the veterinarian for an overall examination. More importantly, they wanted him checked for a microchip that might give them some information about his previous life. They waited nervously in the vet's waiting room, Gabe snuggled against their legs. Finally the vet appeared with the information that Gabe did, indeed, have a microchip. It was reported that his owners, an elderly couple, had perished in a freeway accident days before he had appeared to them. There was no information about how he came to be a stray. Apprehensively, they contacted the older couple's family. No one was interested in having Gabe. They were assured that he was theirs if they wanted him. The search for his former owners had been a trying time, but now they breathed a sigh of relief.

Maggie and Allie spent long days investigating neighborhoods, answering ads, networking with friends trying to find a new home for Allie. Finally, they found an acceptable place in Santa Monica. They moved in with only sleeping bags and a change of clothes each. The next several days were spent in almost frantic shopping. Allie needed everything. Maggie replaced only as much as she needed to get her back to Florida. The Southern California community rallied around the fire victims, offering free food and discounts on most things needed by them. Everywhere they went they were treated with compassion and generosity.

Max LaCroix appeared on their doorstep with his arms filled with kitchen equipment. He and Harry Cavanaugh were frequent visitors to the new apartment. On Harry's first visit he brought flowers. Upon finding that there was no vase for them, he left and returned with three flower vases. At dinner one evening he solemnly presented them with a packet of photos. *The* photos. Harry had picked them up at the Malibu drugstore. Maggie and Allie were shuffling through them as fast as they could. He smiled grimly and said, "Look at the one taken at the airport." They found it and stared, holding it first close to their eyes and then far away. It showed Allie, her face averted, but with sunlight shining off her hair.

With a note of wonder in her voice, Maggie said, "But I can't see anything except Allie. The limo is out of focus and nothing can be seen inside it. All of that for nothing!"

They sat in a stunned silence for a while, then Allie said, "No, Mom. Not for nothing. If you hadn't taken the photo, if John Albright hadn't felt threatened by it, if we hadn't gone through what we did, eight hundred young people might not be here in January. Mom, with that snapshot you saved eight hundred lives."

Allie's friends organized a house warming party for her on the night before Maggie's departure. Over thirty people brought practical gifts that expressed their love and caring for Allie.

The next morning Maggie woke early and looked around Allie's new 'house'. It was a duplex apartment, larger and newer than Allie's Malibu house. Maggie lay in her sleeping bag on the soft off-white carpet in front of the green marble fireplace. Upstairs in the loft bedroom Allie slept in her sleeping bag. The high vaulted ceiling contained several large skylights that made the apartment light and airy. At the very end of the long living room was a well-equipped kitchen. Under the stairs was a bathroom. Across the room stood a huge bird-of-paradise "tree" in sculpture-like splendor. A folding table and two wicker chairs stood in the dining area. A sofa and a bed were to be delivered tomorrow.

Maggie wondered about Allie. Would she and Ed turn their relationship into friendship only? What about Max LaCroix? He still hadn't remembered Allie from the beach. The two of them seemed to strike sparks off of each other. Clearly Max was intrigued by Allie. Where would their friendship lead? Wherever, whatever, Maggie felt that Allie's feet were firmly on the ground.

Yes, Allie would be okay. Gabe was a true gift. It was a relief to know that he was rightfully hers. It seemed that he was heaven sent to help Allie through this time. The effects of the trauma and the loss would be with her for a while, but she'd be all right. Maggie breathed a soft sigh of satisfaction. Maybe she could return in a couple of months and help Allie with the finishing touches. It is strange, she thought, that we take our material world for granted. Really, it is just stuff. But the stuff forms a sort of supportive cocoon from which we order our lives.

Maggie's thoughts turned to Hadi. Who was he really? What a mysterious character he was! In a sense he had served as a sort of guardian angel during their escape from the big white house. Some of what he said and did had seemed almost magical. Strange. Would she ever see him again? He had said so. What about the dream of him on the night of the fire? It was a dream of warning—he told her to leave. Was that what he meant by seeing her again? But, how silly to think like that! Magical thinking!

Harry Cavanaugh. Maggie smiled when she thought about Harry. He had been very present since the fire. But Harry's life was in Los Angeles and Maggie's life in Florida was waiting. He really hadn't talked to her about the future or even about seeing her again after she returned to Florida. It's the old long-distance relationship problem. Whatever happens, he is a sweet man and he has been a good friend. I am richer for knowing him.

Before starting for the airport Allie drove Maggie up the PCH a short distance, not to the area of the fire, but just to look at the ocean. As they passed the old Getty, Maggie looked up with longing and resignation. Well, she thought, maybe next time!

The Miata had been repainted and fitted with a new top. It looked shiny and good as new as they drove to the airport. Allie turned to her mother, "Mom, I don't know how to say thank you for all you've done." Tears welled up in two sets of eyes. "I couldn't have gone through this without you."

Maggie grinned through her tears, "Honey, I don't think you would've had to go through quite all of this if it hadn't been for me and my camera! And I don't know what I'd have done without you. You were wonderful throughout the whole thing. Thank *you*."

Allie smiled at her mother, "I guess we're a pretty good team, huh?"

Maggie dabbed a wandering tear, "Yeah, a pretty good team! I love you, Sweetie."

Allie squeezed her mother's hand, "Yeah, me too. Love you, Mom."

Made in the USA
Lexington, KY
08 December 2009